HEIGHTENED
PROJECT EVOLVE

KEVIN E. MORRIS

Four Apples Publishing
First Paperback Edition: March 2025

Cover Design by Ei
Edited by Elle Arby

ISBN: 979-8-218-63849-8

To Lindsey, Finn, and Emmett.

CHAPTER 1
UP IN SMOKE

"Ah, good morning Mr. Chapman. I heard we had another episode," Doctor Clemens said disapprovingly.

"I just fell asleep for a bit during math class," I said apologetically. "It won't happen again." I don't know when *my* episodes became *our* episodes, but it seemed like a bad idea to say that out loud.

He made a noncommittal noise before picking up a laminated sheet of paper with questions printed on it. He went through the same questions every time I saw him, and wrote my responses in a notebook with my name on the cover.

He had been taking notes in this notebook ever since I came to Hope Street ten years ago. Nothing makes you feel more self-conscious than having someone write down everything you say to them, as you say it. I asked to read his notes a few times through the years, but he was very clear that his notes -about me- were not for me to see.

Diagnosing me with something called Dissociative Amnesia is the only time he truly helped me.

I went to the public library the next day to learn everything I could about the condition. I found a news article about a patient who regained her memory after smelling her husband's cologne. For over a year, I had tried to trigger my memories from a scent, but the only thing that came back to me was fists. My classmates did not appreciate me smelling their belongings.

Doctor Clemens asked me a few questions about my sleeping habits and I told him about my most recent nightmare.

"Ah, still happening then." He made a tsking sound while writing in that journal. "Have you been doing your memory work?"

"Yep," I said, my mouth popping. I had been clearing my mind and focusing on tiny details like the color of the man's eyes or the temperature in the room, but I still could not remember anything about my life prior to being dropped at Hope Street at five years old.

"And," he prompted.

"Still just a man kneeling in front of me to say something before he left me with the headmaster."

"We still don't remember what he said, or what he looked like?"

"No." I knew he was frustrated that I couldn't remember, but I was definitely *more* frustrated about not remembering my own life.

He glanced at the clock, closed his notebook, and stood. This was his cue for me to leave. I gladly took it, slinging my backpack over one shoulder and making my way to the dining room.

The hallways were chaotic as my classmates shoved their way towards dinner. It was like watching a herd of cattle rush the stockades, and I had to choose between joining the stampede or being trampled by it.

I was pushed from every direction. The biggest and most aggressive kids wanted to be front and center, so I wanted to be anywhere *except* front and center. The safest option for me was to get to the outside of the group and walk along the wall.

I took my tray and offered the cafeteria chef a grateful smile before making my way out of the crowded room. If anybody noticed me, which I doubted, it would look like I was headed to the dormitories on the top floor.

Walking past my room, I found the large "restricted" sign at the end of the hallway. I stuck my arm through the gate, feeling around until I found the deadbolt.

Once I located the lock with my pinky finger, I shifted my hand so that the hairpin I was holding between my thumb and index finger would slide into the keyhole.

I had a collection of hair pins that I found at the park over the past few years and could pick most of the locks in the building if I had enough time. This one, however, was as familiar to me as my own hand. I smiled as the bolt slid out of the hole, and I pulled the lock free.

After locking the gate behind me, I made sure to put the hairpin back in my pocket.

Holding my tray in one hand, I wrapped my arm around the side of the ladder and climbed.

When I was twelve, we had a new teacher who wanted to teach us 'life skills'. She built a greenhouse on the roof to teach us about growing our own food, taught us how to balance a bank account, and even took us into the kitchens to learn how to cook pasta.

We all loved the class but, like most things at Hope Street, it didn't last. She left after a few months and none of the teachers after her bothered to keep up the lessons.

I made my way to the old greenhouse on the far side of the roof and watered the plants before plopping down beside the stack of books that I had taken from the "free" bin outside of the city library.

I set my dinner tray on top of the book pile and made myself comfortable.

I took small bites. Focusing on the taste and texture of the food helped me forget about my day, and gave me a few minutes of peace. It also helped distract me from the way our food looked.

The food almost never looked appealing, but it always tasted delicious. Our chef was the best thing about Hope Street. He had been here as long as me and didn't show any signs of burning out.

When I finished my dinner, I checked the time. I still had nearly an hour until sunset. I needed to get new books from the library, but I would do that another day. Today I just wanted to stand at the edge of the roof and watch normal people on the street below me. It was easy to imagine a life in the real world; drinking coffee, laughing with friends, rushing to school or work or appointments.

A family.

A home.

No boring math classes.

No Doctor Clemens.

Just happiness.

The image of my perfect life was torn from my grasp as sounds of anarchy reached me. My classmates' voices were loud enough that I could make out a few words from the roof.

"Get him!"

"Fight!"

"Get up!"

Dillon must have found a new victim. I hoped he was losing the fight.

A shiver ran up my spine and I realized that the sun had set while I was daydreaming. I grabbed the sweatshirt from my backpack and laid down for my favorite part of the night.

Bundled in my sweatshirt, I searched for constellations until I found it hard to keep my eyes open. Shuffling from the exhaustion of staring up at Cassiopeia and Andromeda for a few hours, I snuck past the security guard and into my dark room.

I kicked off my shoes and collapsed into bed, falling asleep immediately.

It didn't last long.

It never did.

"Help! Please! Help us!" A woman screamed for help, her voice hysterical.

A man sputtered and gasped for air, the chaotic sounds of splashing water growing fainter along with his breath.

Footsteps crunched quickly across gravelly sand, accompanied by the faint sound of flapping.

"Please! My dad," the woman howled. "He was swimming, but" her voice trailed off, breaking into a sob.

The flapping footsteps raced across the sand as the woman's sobs transformed to weepy prayers for whatever or whoever was listening to save her father.

The sound of running feet was replaced by quick, determined splashes. The steady rhythm of splashing stopped for a moment, then became uneven, like the swimmer was only using half of their body.

Something tumbled, falling hard onto the sand.

The woman's desperate prayers were replaced by swift, small footsteps and sobs as an old man gasped for air.

"It's okay Dad, an ambulance is on the way," she said in a too-loud panic.

"Thank you so much, si-" her hoarse voice grew suddenly loud again.
"Sir?"
"Sir!"

My entire body was covered in sweat. Again.

Most people only have occasional nightmares. I have them every night. When I was younger, I came up with the term blaremares for mine; horrible dreams that only involve sound.

I laid in bed, staring at the blackness around me as I willed my heart to slow down.

My sweat had dried into a fine layer of itchy salt by the time I fell asleep again. I had barely begun to dream.

A child whimpered as wood crackled loudly in a fire.

The sharp pops of burning wood echoed inside my head and brought me fully back to consciousness. It sounded so real.

Afraid my brain would continue that plotline if I fell back asleep, I sat up and leaned against the wall until my racing heart slowed down for the second time that night.

When my exhausted body started to melt back towards the bed, I laid down again and closed my eyes. I hoped that I would have a dreamless sleep, but my eyes shot open when I realized that I could still hear the crackling wood.

I jumped up, pulling the cord to turn on my light. I didn't see any signs of fire. No smoke. No bright lights.

I opened my door to check the hallway, but only saw the crisp red emergency light. No smoke or bright lights there either.

I could feel the sound of a fire pulsing through my body, like sitting too close to a loud speaker at the park.

Happy that I had fallen asleep with all of my clothes on, I snuck down the hallway.

The night security guard usually took his nap between 2:00am and 4:00am. Silence meant I would have a successful escape.

I made my way down the hallway, listening at each door for signs that there might be a fire inside each room. When I reached the other end of the hallway, I realized that the sound was coming from outside the building.

I passed under the emergency light, tiptoed down the stairs, and eased the door open.

Standing just outside the back door, I picked up a small rock and pushed it into the door jamb to prevent the door from locking me out.

I slowly eased the door closed, to make sure the rock would stay put. Then I ran.

My feet carried me towards a quiet neighborhood with perfectly manicured lawns.

The smell of smoke grew stronger with every step.

I turned a corner and stopped so abruptly that I almost tripped over my own feet.

A man stood in the middle of the road cradling a small girl in his arms. Their silhouette was backlit by the glowing wood beams of what I could only assume used to be their home.

Several firefighters spoke quietly with one another, gesturing towards various areas of the house, while a few others sprayed water into the pile of embers. I could see from the ash smeared across their faces that they had been there for a while.

Sweat dripped from their brows as they tirelessly worked to ensure that the fire didn't spread to the rest of the houses on the street. I glanced at those homes and realized that most of the neighbors were standing on their porches, watching the fire slowly die.

Between the fire and the water hose, everything had been destroyed except a pink bunny held tightly in the hands of the little girl. A girl who was crying.

I suddenly couldn't hear anything as my brain tried to process the possibility that I had heard this scene from my room… inside a building and over a mile away.

My heart raced and I found my breaths coming in short.

Afraid I was having another panic attack, I tried to clear my brain and focus on filling my lungs.

In.

Out.

In.

Out.

I rolled my shoulders and continued taking slow breaths as I watched one of the neighbors walk into the road to wrap a blanket around the man and his daughter.

I knew the panic attack had passed when my body began to register other sensations.

My hands stung from the cold night air. I shook them out and flexed my fingers in an attempt to warm them.

The acrid smell of wet smoke filled my nostrils so thoroughly that I could taste it in the back of my throat.

Pebbles crunched against the pavement behind me.

I turned my head to the side, catching the shape of a man in my periphery.

I turned more fully, watching him retreat. He wore all black; black tracksuit, black baseball hat, tattered black shoes. One of the soles had come partially undone, flipping open and closed with each step like a little mouth.

The constant flap vaguely reminded me of something.

A song I heard at the park? I mentally ran through the sounds I normally heard; the cotton candy vendor, the ducks, runners and bicyclists, an occasional boom box. Maybe something from Hope Street?

With that thought, my stomach sank. I had no idea what time it was. The last time a student was caught sneaking out at night, he had detention for a month.

I ran all the way back to Hope Street, hoping I wouldn't smell like smoke. Leaning against the back wall next to the open door, I caught my breath. Once I was confident with my ability to be quiet, I slowly pulled the door open and nudged the rock back into the street using my toes.

As I walked up the stairs, I worried about what was happening to me. It just wasn't possible to hear a little girl crying from my bedroom over a mile away. Maybe some weather phenomenon was pushing sound waves along an invisible current, and I just happened to sleep in the middle of its path.

Reaching the top of the stairs, I turned the corner to my hallway and stopped dead under the red emergency light.

I was so engrossed in my thoughts that I had forgotten about the night security guard, who was standing with his back to me. I was so close that I would be able to touch him on the shoulder if I extended my arm.

Holding my breath, I took two cautious steps backwards and pivoted into the stairwell.

With my back against the wall, I listened to him grunt and crack his knuckles.

If my heart beat any harder, it was going to fly out of my chest.

After what felt like years, I heard his footsteps receding down the hallway.

I dared to peek around the corner. He had stopped at the other end and was just standing there checking his phone.

"Go! Go! Go!" I mentally screamed, willing him to take the last few steps so that I would have a clear shot to my door.

He bobbed his head up and down a few times before tucking his phone into his back pocket and turning the corner.

My eyes darted from my door to the corner he had disappeared behind, and I mentally calculated the odds of him coming back down this hallway. After doing a quick check to make sure he didn't leave anything behind, I sprinted to my door and threw myself into bed.

Running my hands down my face, I laughed. I couldn't believe that I hadn't gotten caught, and I felt giddy as I mentally replayed my close call. For once, I was grateful to have my own room. Then I remembered that I had my own room because nobody else would put up with my constant blaremares, which further reminded me of the reason I left my room in the first place.

I sobered up as I thought about the fire. I could smell the smoke in my hair, and would need to wash it in the morning to make sure I got the stench out, but my clothes seemed fine.

I spent the remainder of the night trying to make sense of the fire. I shouldn't have been able to hear something so far away. Maybe something was wrong, and I couldn't differentiate between what was real and what was not real any longer.

I had never been so confused.

Or scared.

Saturday morning was a relief. Being surrounded by a room full of my classmates sounded like torture after the events of last night. At least today I would be able to leave Hope Street through the front door.

I found myself sitting at the park, watching a man teach his son how to fly a kite. Before I discovered my rooftop oasis at Hope Street, I came to the park in hopes of finding my parents. Naive, right? Like they would drop me at Hope Street and then hang out at the park across the street. Ridiculous.

I watched as intact families walked past me, and I imagined what life would look like if they were mine.

When I was ten, I broke into the headmaster's office to snoop for information about my parents. It didn't take long to read my student file. While the other boys' files were thick with documents, mine only held a few old report cards.

Pushing that memory down, I sat on the park bench until long after the wind died down and the little boy put away his kite. The possibilities and impossibilities of last night made me more confused the more I thought about them.

I considered that I might have dreamed the entire thing, but that didn't explain the faint smoky smell that clung to my hair even after I had scrubbed myself raw in the shower.

I wondered if I was psychic, my foresight beckoning me to a fire that I could hear before it ignited. Maybe I was able to telepathically hear what other people heard, and I just heard the fire through the mind of the little girl or her father.

None of my theories were logical, but neither were the events of last night.

I snapped back to reality when the bench shifted under the weight of somebody next to me. The subtle bump interrupted my thoughts and ruined my mood.

Frustrated that this person had chosen to invade my personal space instead of sitting on one of the dozens of empty benches, I reached down to snatch my backpack from under the bench so I could leave.

As my fingers grazed the straps of the bag, I saw my benchmate's shoes.

Old, tattered black shoes; the soles nearly worn through.

My mind and heart raced as I jerked back up and found the man calmly watching me. I froze under the weight of his stare. Deer in headlights had nothing on me as his eyes seemed to penetrate my soul; the eyes of the man who had brought me to Hope Street.

"Hello Kai. We need to talk." He gave me a meaningful look, then turned and walked away.

CHAPTER 2
TATTERED BLACK SHOES

I followed this man, maybe my father, across the park. We came to a cotton candy vendor who proceeded to swirl sugary blue clouds onto a stick, blissfully unaware of the absolute crisis I was experiencing.

The man tore off a large piece of the fluffy sugar and shoved it into his mouth, smiling softly. An errant thought danced through my brain; if this man wasn't my father, he could be a serial killer. Like a real, murder-y serial killer with a mask and a knife and a lair full of bodies and…

Slap

Slap

Slap

He casually walked along the path, eating his spun sugar.

No. No, no, no, no, no.

My throat closed up.

I struggled to breathe as I thought about how impossible it would be for me to have dreamed about him walking on a beach, seen him at a house fire, and now he claims to know me.

Did I dream him into reality? Was I currently hallucinating?

Was my desperation so potent that it created a real person to give me the answers I want?

"Wait," I croaked.

I steeled myself and shouted, though my voice still came out rough.

"Hey!"

He turned his head to the side, acknowledging that he heard me without pausing to slow down or respond.

"Stop!" I found myself running to catch up with him.

I kept going until I was slightly ahead of him, then turned so I was standing directly in his path.

"What are you," I demanded.

My heart raced in a combination of physical exertion and panic, and I could feel the blood pounding throughout my entire body.

He cocked his head, studying me. He quietly stared at me until I shifted my weight and adjusted my shirt uncomfortably.

I amended my question.

"Who are you?"

"Flint."

"Ok, Flint." I was glad to have a name, but I wanted to know who he was in the grander sense. I took a deep breath and quickly cataloged all of the questions I had for him; sorting them by immediate importance.

"Are you my dad?" I tried to keep the hope out of my voice, though I'm not sure whether I succeeded or not.

"No, I am not."

"Okay, am I in trouble?" I was beginning to feel nervous.

He looked down, pursing his lips.

"You have done nothing wrong."

"Okay, so I'm not in trouble," I started before he started speaking again.

"I didn't say that."

What was that supposed to mean? Was he trying to push me over the edge?

"Did I," I trailed off, realizing that asking somebody if you dreamed them into reality would be very rude if the answer was 'no'. And I was pretty sure the answer was 'no'.

"Your name is Flint. How did you know my name is Kai?"

"I have known you since you were b…"

He froze, his eyes going unfocused. "I have a lot to tell you, but we can't talk here. Is there a private place where you feel safe, or would you like me to find a place?"

It felt like a joke. A not-very-funny joke, punctuated by a large piece of cotton candy being shoved into his mouth.

I started to suspect that he was a detective. Maybe he thought I started the house fire. But then, why wouldn't he bring me to 'the station' like they did in movies? And he already said I didn't do anything wrong.

"Why can't we talk here?" I looked around pointedly. It was late afternoon. The families had all gone home for the day, but the runners hadn't come out yet. The park was nearly deserted.

"You need to know what you are, Kai. It would be very," he paused, tilting his head side to side a few times, "unsafe if somebody overheard."

He said "what". Not "who".

I am a "what".

I suddenly found it hard to stand. I flopped to the ground, still blocking his path, and focused on bringing air into my lungs. My vision went a bit fuzzy around the edges as I looked at his ratty slap-slap shoes.

He squatted down so that he was nearly at eye level with me.

I have never seen anybody look so serious.

This man; he knew what was wrong with me.

I felt my entire body breaking into a million pieces. Cell by cell. Torn apart.

He pulled a small water bottle from his jacket and offered it to me.

I took it without thinking and emptied the contents in three big gulps, only realizing afterwards that it could have been poisoned.

He seemed to notice the realization on my face as I stared at the empty bottle.

"It's just water, I promise."

He continued squatting in front of me, his head tilted to the side and his eyes going in and out of focus, until my breathing evened out.

The man - Flint - stood and offered his hand to me.

My entire body shivered uncontrollably, but I was able to stand without accepting the help he was offering.

"How do I know you won't hurt me?"

"If I wanted to hurt you, I would have done it last night; not within throwing distance of your school." He pointed to Hope Street, but I didn't turn my head to look. I knew where it was.

I looked down, steeling myself for what I hoped was the right decision.

Raising my head, I looked him dead in the eyes.

"Meet me at the back door in twenty minutes."

Before I could change my mind, I turned on my heel and walked unsteadily back to Hope Street.

He was waiting for me when I opened the back door; lips stained blue from his cotton candy.

Hope Street served dinner early on weekends, providing the distraction Flint and I needed in order to get to my greenhouse without being seen.

I plopped down, grabbing a blanket.

"Safe space to talk," I gestured vaguely around me, then sat quietly waiting for him to fill the silence.

"Your name is Kai. My name is Flint," he began.

I opened my mouth to tell him that I already knew this information, but he held his hand up to stop me before any words came out.

"I worked with your parents. When you were born, I promised them that I would help you and keep you safe if something hap…"

I scoffed. Loudly. How had he helped me? I had never even seen him before, and my life at Hope Street had been, well, terrible.

As indignant as I felt, he stared me down until I was cowed into silence.

"Your father, Carter, was my best friend. He was murdered along with Katherine; your mother."

Carter.

Katherine.

I tried to listen, but my entire world shifted at the knowledge of my parents' names.

"The people responsible would have come for you next. I had very few choices to keep you off their radar. Hope Street, however you feel about it, did keep you safe. Until recently."

"Recently?" I asked dryly. I thought of all the times kids like Dillon had left bruises on me and wondered how my parents would have reacted if they had seen the way it was here.

"It was relatively safe until a few weeks ago. It's becoming less safe for you every day."

"Okay," I let out a sigh, "Why is it suddenly not safe here?"

He sat and patted the bench next to him. My eyes slid to the bench, but I made no move to stand.

"The Heightened worked with the most elite teams in every branch of government; CIA, FBI, Secret Service, even some departments that were so secret they didn't have names."

"So you were in this Heightened group with my dad? Carter? What did your group do?" My voice came out weaker than I would have liked, especially because I was finally getting information that I had been searching for ever since I could remember. Information that the headmaster refused to tell me. Information that wasn't in my student file.

He scowled. "The correct question would be 'Who are the Heightened?' Some people have a fast metabolism. Some people have quick reflexes. Some people have an enhanced sense of sight, smell, taste, touch, or hearing. Some people, like us, have all of these things."

"Okay, so you and your group are," I searched for the word, "athletic?"

"Me and my *group*," he laughed. "Your father, your mother, and, well, you would be included in that category. And we are a bit more than 'athletic'. Most of us have senses much stronger than a typical person. Some of us have senses that you would consider to be magical or supernatural; hearing and seeing things that should be impossible."

"Civilians," he waved his hand down towards the park, which was starting to fill with runners and dog walkers, "were happily ignorant for hundreds of years, except for a small number of government leaders who oversaw our assignments. Then they turned on us."

"Who turned on you? The entire government?" I asked. He was starting to sound like a conspiracy theorist, which meant he was almost definitely not seeing the world clearly. I shifted slightly away from him.

Flint gave a heavy sigh.

"These heightened senses are passed down genetically; parent to child. A few of our younger members did not want to work in covert operations. They wanted to be athletes, musicians, artists, police, or just normal people. These kids just wanted to choose their own destiny, but our handlers were afraid that a Heightened with their own desires would be a threat to global security. They only saw us as weapons to wield.

"One of our handlers, Stratus, had received dozens of awards for his work in war prevention and political extraction. Of course, all of his operations were carried out by teams of Heightened. We worked side by side until he noticed that some of our children had dreams of their own. He became terrified of what an unbound Heightened could mean for his mission."

Flint looked me directly in the eyes. "Frightened people with power are the most dangerous thing on this planet."

I rocked back and looked to the ground as I pieced together the things Flint had said.

Somebody, probably this Stratus guy, killed my parents because he was afraid of children.

He would have killed me - a child - in order to prevent me from having free will.

My parents didn't leave me here because I was unwanted.

Flint did. He left me here. To keep me alive.

When I felt ready to hear more, I looked back up at him and braced myself.

"What happened?"

Flint held my gaze, chewing on the inside of his cheeks until he was satisfied with whatever he saw.

"He requested a meeting with all of us on New Years Eve. We were supposed to discuss the options that would be available to the children who did not want to work in covert operations. My partner and his wife were there. I stayed home to watch their son so that they could go out and celebrate after the meeting. At midnight, when the whole city was celebrating, the building exploded."

"Stratus and his men are the only people who survived that meeting. I don't know how. I don't even know if he bothered to show up to the meeting before murdering everybody, or if he simply pushed a button from the comfort of his bedroom."

Flint tilted his head side to side, stretching his neck, before rolling his shoulders back and continuing.

"After that, he came for the rest of us, one by one. Stratus didn't know that my partner had a son. When he found out that I had survived, I became their next target. I tried to keep the boy safe with me, but running for your life is no way for a child to live. I brought the boy to the only safe place I knew about."

He swept his hand down, indicating the building below us.

"I brought him to Hope Street."

As if I needed him to spell it out. I knew he was talking about me. Did he think I was still that child he left behind? He continued talking, explaining the process of leaving "that boy" with the headmaster, but all I could do was stare at him blankly while my brain flew through a million images of my parents being blown up.

"There were so many times that I wanted to explain this to you, but I knew it wouldn't be safe for either of us. Each time I came back to check on you required months of preparation. I would circle this city for months to ensure that I wasn't being followed, and once I knew it was safe, I could only stay for a few hours to ensure…"

"Do you have a picture? Of my parents, I mean." I didn't care that I was interrupting him.

"No, unfortunately not, but I do know somebody who does. I hoped to have more time before you needed me, but last night I realized that your abilities are developing too quickly. Somebody is going to notice. When I followed you to the fire last night, I knew we had run out of time. You need to leave Hope Street. If you come with me, I will make sure you see the photos."

Overwhelmed with information, I responded with the only thing I had: sarcasm.

"So my parents were murdered, the government wants to kill me because I'm a mutant, and you thought Hope Street would be a good place for me to grow up? And now, I'm supposed to go with you to meet your 'friend' who has something I want? I have heard the stories. I don't need to take a ride in a candy van to know what happens next." I finished, my tone biting.

"I know this is a lot to take in, but right now you need to come with me. I can explain everything else in time," Flint said.

"A lot to take," I cut off, scoffing. "Yeah, it's a bit much to 'take in'," I said as rudely as I could muster.

"I mean, I have the reflexes of a sloth, so obviously I have special powers," I said sarcastically. "You clearly make good decisions like leaving a child at Hope Street to spend their entire life thinking their parents abandoned them, so I'd *love* to go somewhere with you."

"Not all of your abilities will develop at the same rate. It would take years to understand all of your gifts, and many more years to be able to control them." He clenched his jaw. "I will make this promise to you: Kai Chapman, if you come with me, I will take you to a place where Stratus will never find you."

I started to respond, but he continued talking over me. "Think back on the time where you were at your calmest. In those moments, you heard or felt something you couldn't explain. What brought you to the fire last night?"

I sat in stunned silence for a moment. I was unsure how to respond, so I stood up and began running. I could hear Flint hollering for me to stop but I just didn't care. I had to get away.

I ran as fast as my feet could go; back down to the dormitory floor, and into my closet of a room. I pushed my small dresser up against the door in an attempt to blockade it.

I wish I could forget everything Flint told me. Satisfied that I had made myself as safe as possible, I collapsed on my bed.

I felt something tickling my jaw. When I brushed it off, my hand came away wet. I hadn't even realized that I was crying until then.

I rolled over, facing away from the door and attempted some of the relaxation strategies I had worked on with the school counselor, on the rare occasion that she was at Hope Street and not busy redirecting kids like Dillon.

When my feelings had stopped leaking out of me and my heart rate had returned to normal, I mentally prioritized the main points that Flint had shared.

The most time sensitive question was: Is a man from the government on his way to kill me?

If the answer was yes, my next question was: Am I more safe with Flint or without him?

If everything Flint said was true, Stratus was smart enough to trick an entire group of people, and murder them without consequence. Surely he would find me eventually.

If Flint was lying, well, it didn't feel like he was lying.

It felt absolutely ridiculous, but maybe the voices in my head had been real the entire time.

For the first time in my life, I actually tried to listen.

At first I heard nothing. Then, slowly, I could hear noises that came from outside my room. Like the groaning of the headmaster's chair as he shifted his weight, and the wind chimes from the cat lady's porch who lived across the street. My body went still as I used all of my remaining energy to focus on the noises. I heard the hum of the park vendor's cotton candy machine.

I could never do that before.

I wondered if I could do this my whole life, and if so, whether I would have ever realized it without Flint telling me what was happening to my body.

As I listened, the sounds became vague pictures I could see in my head.

I saw little kids laughing at the candy store, their scoopers scraping across candy as they filled their bags.

Then I saw Flint, standing behind Hope Street, motionless except for his index finger which was tapping against his leg.

I sat up and looked towards my barricaded door. I didn't know how he had managed to get from the roof to the street.

I was very certain that he had more information about me, and I was mostly certain that he wanted to help me, even if he had a history of 'helping' in very unhelpful ways.

I walked down the staircase and opened the door.

"Tell me everything," I demanded.

His fingers stopped the steady rhythm and he lowered his eyes towards mine. "I will," he said.

He handed me a small bottle of apple juice. "Your blood sugar is dropping too fast. You have six minutes to drink this, pack your things, and meet me here. I have already been here for too long."

This time I drank without wondering whether it was poisoned.

CHAPTER 3
ROAD TRIP

Though Flint assured me that we were mostly headed in the right direction, we seemed to take a very indirect path towards wherever we were going. I didn't know a lot about the towns we stopped in, but I knew enough to realize that we were not traveling in a straight line.

Flint never told me what to expect next. I don't think he knew himself.

We would spend hours squatting in silence, then quickly travel from subway to car to train, then I would find myself running down alleyways or through peoples' backyards.

When I was allowed to talk, I asked questions. I wanted to know everything. For security, I wasn't allowed to speak names.

"Just in case," he said.

I asked about my parents, the bad guy, the good guys, how the good guys started working for the big thing, if anybody else in the big thing knew about us (other than the bad guy).

Sometimes he gave me brief answers. Sometimes he grunted and told me to ask him again later. Sometimes he told me I wasn't allowed to ask questions because, even speaking in code, the threat was too close.

Each night we found ourselves sleeping in a new location; abandoned buildings, backyard sheds, community parks, unlocked cars, or highway underpasses. Solitude was Flint's only criteria.

One night, we slept in an orange grove. For dinner, we ate the juiciest oranges I had ever tasted.

I never thought I would miss my tiny room back at Hope Street, but at least I had a pillow and a blanket instead of my lumpy backpack and a sweatshirt.

On the fifteenth day, he brought us into a hotel and walked straight to the front desk.

"My son and I have been driving across the country to visit his mother in the hospital," he explained to the teenager at the desk.

"We would like to shower and change, so we can look presentable for her. Is it possible to rent a room for just a few minutes?"

The young woman at the desk looked at me with pity as she accepted his money and handed him the key to our room.

"Take all the time you need, buddy. I'll be rooting for your mom."

It took a lot of self control to keep the surprise off of my face. He lied so effortlessly.

Feeling like a new person after my shower, I sat on the bed and watched TV while Flint took his turn in the bathroom. The newscasters spoke about traffic incidents, the results of various sports games, and local events.

I was relieved to know what city we were in, but it shocked me to see that the world had just carried on after my life had imploded.

We left the hotel with freshly washed hair and clean clothes, and took a taxi across town where Flint bought enough food and water to fill both of our backpacks. As he handed me some of my favorite foods, I wondered when the day's luck was going to run out.

Maybe I jinxed myself, because our next destination was the dirt floor of somebody's garden shed.

After a day and a half, he said it was safe to travel again.

"I haven't heard any of them since yesterday morning. If we leave now, we should be there soon."

"Where are we going?" I had asked him this question several times a day since we left Hope Street, but his answer was always to ask him later.

He lowered his voice and spoke in a deep whisper.

"We are going to a place that we found after the incident. When the survivors were being hunted down, we found a place for all of us to live in safety."

He lowered his voice until it was barely audible, causing me to rely heavily on lip reading, "the Sanctuary."

"Wait, all of us?" I asked loudly, the shock of his statement making me forget to keep my voice quiet.

Flint's eyes bulged at my loudness, reminding me that I was supposed to whisper until we arrived at the destination; this *Sanctuary*. He tilted his head to the side and listened for an incoming threat.

This piece of information was a big deal, and I was practically vibrating with questions as I waited for his eyes to refocus on me, indicating that he was satisfied with our tenuous safety.

"I thought you were the only one left. And me, I guess. And whoever has a photo of my parents."

"Yes, there are other people like us. I only know a few of them, but I am sure there are other good guys who have joined the place by now." Even using our code words, Flint's whisper remained quieter than usual. I found myself leaning closer to him in order to understand all of his words.

"After your parents were gone, the bad guy changed his focus. He wasn't trying to prevent major attacks on civilians; his focus was on striking the enemy -our children- before they became a threat. He organized a team of other bad guys to hunt us down, using our old employee records to go after our family, friends, and contacts.

"Under his direction, they eliminated everybody whom they labeled as an enemy. Once he was satisfied that he had taken all of us out of the picture, he moved his operation out of the shadows. With this, he gained even more money and power to grow his department. Over the past ten years, they have preemptively attacked every perceived threat."

While I had been worried about math tests and tetanus shots at Hope Street, entire towns were wiped from existence because Stratus *suspected* that one Heightened person might live there!

I wondered how this group could kill so many people without raising suspicion, but always a step ahead of me, Flint went on to explain the tactical precision of Stratus's strikes. He was a smart man; he had earned his ranking in the government by knowing the enemy better than anybody else.

Always careful not to draw too much attention, he masked each attack as an accident or natural disaster. Flint told me about the way that the group had contaminated water supplies, started brush fires, caused factory explosions, framed radical groups, and implicated enemy countries to cover up these murders.

I wanted to hear more, but our conversation was cut short by two hard knocks on the door. As the shed rattled and bits of dust gently fell onto our heads, my brain emptied of every thought except, "run!"

I grasped at the floor for anything that could be used as a weapon. Finding only a bag of manure and a small trowel, I sprung to my feet and retreated into the corner of the room with my fists clenched tightly in front of me.

I looked to Flint for guidance on how to save ourselves, but found him merely looking annoyed at the interruption as he walked to the old wooden door.

A tall, slender man stood on the threshold. He wore a long black overcoat, sun-bleached on the shoulders from years of wear. It contrasted with his silver hair, which was long enough to touch his shoulders. He appeared at least ten years older than Flint, but seemed to be just as strong.

He took off his satchel, dropping it unceremoniously onto the dirt at Flint's feet.

Nobody spoke. Both men looked each other up and down, seeming to size each other up. Just as I was beginning to wonder how long this weird staring contest would continue, the other man spoke.

"Well, you look terrible."

Flint's pursed lips gave way to a grin as he embraced the other man in an enthusiastic hug. I took a tentative step forward so I was standing behind Flint.

He broke from the man and gestured towards me.

"This is him."

The man stood for several heartbeats, scrutinizing me from head to toe before heaving a deep breath. "He looks just like Carter," he said to Flint.

His eyes refocused, seeming to realize that he was talking at me rather than to me. "Hello young man, my name is Estes."

"Hello," I squeaked. Embarrassed, I cleared my throat and tried to sound at least marginally more confident than I felt.

"My name is Kai."

It felt like just minutes ago I was sitting on a park bench wondering who I was, and now I had two people right in front of me who held all of the answers.

Flint smiled proudly at me before his eyes slid to the front pocket of Estes's jacket.

"I've been listening to that keychain rattle for weeks. Did you really need to keep it in your pocket?" His voice was gruff, but he still had a smile on his face.

Estes reached into his pocket and brought out an old key chain containing a solitary key. The remnants of an old skeleton key dangled through his fingers, the edges worn smooth from years of use.

"Yes, I did," he responded, smiling down at the keychain in his palm.

"And yes, I have been following you, but I was keeping my distance for your safety. I had two men on my tail, and I had to lose them before I came to you."

"And you're certain they haven't followed you here?" Flint asked casually, though the tension in his shoulders gave away his true feelings.

"They are on their way to China in a shipping crate, so yes, I am confident that they have not followed me here. I have seen a dramatic increase in the number of trackers over the last few months." Estes replied. Then, glancing between me and Flint, he lowered his voice. "They are becoming more persistent. He must be preparing for something."

"That's why it is so important for us to get back. All of us. We have to tell the rest of them what is happening out here," said Flint.

It was the first time that Flint had spoken openly about our plans. It helped to have another person around who understood Flint. I doubted that Flint would have spoken so openly if it was just me and him.

I felt a wave of longing wash over me. I grew up knowing nothing about my parents, and now I was in a room with two people who knew them personally. Maybe the two people in the whole world who knew them best.

I was excited at the possibility of learning about my parents, my past, and this Sanctuary place. As I listened to Flint and Estes share the details of what they had been working on since they had last seen each other, I realized my questions could wait. I was already learning more about the Heightened just by listening to them.

Before Stratus killed most of the Heightened, Estes was the liaison between Stratus's agency and the Heightened team. Estes spoke of Stratus with a mixture of respect and absolute hatred. The mere mention of his name caused both men to steer to a different topic. After catching up, they reminisced about previous missions. I fell asleep around midnight, listening as they laughed and spoke fondly of their previous work together.

By sunrise, we were hiding in a freight car on the back of a train. When I was nine, my class at Hope Street had taken a train to the zoo, and I had enthusiastically watched the passing scenery through the window. This was different. There were no windows. I stole glances through a crack in the sliding door, but there was nothing to see except for sand.

I could only imagine where we were headed. Even cacti seemed to have trouble growing in the terrain. I was beginning to understand how the other Heightened were able to forego capture all these years. Nothing should be able to survive in such a desolate and lifeless place.

The train slowed to go around a bend in the tracks, and we took the opportunity to jump off into the sand. After the dust settled and the sound of the train's engine disappeared, we were left with an unsettling calm. There were no sounds of life, just the wind causing the sand to scrape against itself.

Estes took a deep breath, looking pleased. "Just like I remember."

His remark confused me. There were no landmarks of any kind to pinpoint our location.

"How do you know where we are?" I asked.

"Listen," said Flint.

I closed my eyes and heard nothing.

"You're not listening," Flint scolded me. "Listen like you would at night. Go past what you think is possible. Only then can you realize your full potential."

I closed my eyes again and focused on the sand moving across the ground with nothing in the way to stop it. Once I was familiar with the sound, I pushed harder; listened deeper. Suddenly, there was a hint of noise that hadn't been there before. It came from deep below us and was trying to make its way to the surface. I listened closer and closer as the sound became clearer.

Humans. A whole group of them. In the middle of the desert.

I could not make out their words over the sound of rushing water. Water!

Out here in the middle of a blisteringly hot desert, we stood on the white sand while other humans and water were underneath us.

In my excitement, I lost my focus and my hearing snapped back to the faint sound of wind blowing past us. I tried to listen again but nothing came. I knelt, pressing my hands against the hot desert floor. Jaw clenched, I closed my eyes and reached deep inside myself for some shred of the power and focus I had felt moments ago.

Discouraged, I hung my head. It was useless.

I felt a hand on my shoulder and turned my head to see Estes smiling down at me.

"It will come." He was so casual about it, like he had seen this a hundred times. Maybe he had, back when they weren't living under the desert.

Estes's conviction gave me a small bit of confidence, but I still could not shake the feeling of failure as I began walking with them. I didn't like being 'bad' at things, and I was *very* bad at controlling this power.

At least I understood why we were hours away from any manner of civilization.

We walked in the scorching heat for another hour, as if there was a secret road only visible to them.

"Finally," Flint said as sweat poured down his face. It was so hot that the sweat on his shirt dried the moment it started to show.

Estes gave me a secret smile before approaching a small rock piling that looked like every other one that we passed. I watched as Flint followed Estes into one of the cracks. Flint brushed one of the walls with his hand, clearing the loose sand away.

Once he was satisfied with his sand removal, he stepped to the side and gestured grandly to Estes. Estes pulled out his noisy keychain and looked back to me as he slid the key into one of the hundreds of small crevices in the rock.

"You ready?" He twisted the key.

"I ran out of water ten minutes ago and the sun won't set for another few hours. If it takes us out of this heat, I will go anywhere." What I didn't say out loud was that I really hoped this place had air conditioning.

I heard a light click, then an entire boulder shifted up. It moved just enough for us to squeeze underneath it, and I watched as Estes then Flint crawled through. Afraid the giant rock would slam down on top of me, I tossed my backpack through and backed up so I could get a running start before I threw myself through the hole.

Once inside, Flint raised an eyebrow at me before releasing a lever. The rock slid back into place so slowly that I felt my cheeks flush in embarrassment at how ridiculous I must have looked as I shot through the small opening.

He reached down to retrieve an oil lantern from the floor. Flipping open his Zippo lighter like an old movie star, he lit the wick. The chamber lit up, showing that we were at one end of a very long tunnel, which sloped downwards into blackness.

Flint and Estes seemed to have no trouble finding their way down the tunnel in complete darkness. Flint handed me the lantern and I held it out in front of me as I followed behind them, keeping my right hand on the wall for balance.

The temperature cooled as we made our way down, and I was grateful for the reprieve. I took off my baseball hat to feel the cold breeze on my sweat-drenched hair, and attached it to my backpack so I could keep my hand on the wall. The sandy rock under my hand slowly transformed into lush green vines, then to dark rock as smooth as glass.

The voices became louder with each step we took, echoing down the corridor and funneling directly into my ears. It was strange to think that these were the voices I had heard an hour before.

We turned a corner, giving me a glimpse of light at the end of the tunnel. I snuffed out the lantern as we approached a brilliantly lit room. My eyes were still adjusting to the newfound light as a crowd of people swarmed around us. Questions were being thrown at us left and right.

"How are you?"

"Where have you been?"

"Who is the boy?"

"Any news?"

As we wove our way through the chaos, Flint and Estes responded to each question as quickly as it was thrown at us. Over one hundred people in the cave seemed just as surprised to see us as I was to see all of them.

It's not every day that you happen upon a secret underground society in the desert.

They made great use of their tiny space by building across the floor and up to the ceiling. The vines provided a lattice along the walls, which were in turn covered with plant-based hammocks and ladders. Above the hammocks, thin bridges connected small rooms that had been carved into the walls of the cave.

There were no safety harnesses or railings to prevent the inhabitants from falling fifty feet to their death, but these people seemed to have no problem navigating the deadly walkways and ladders. Even small children were swinging from ropes and vines, or tightrope walking from one hammock to another. It was as if these people had never heard the words "be careful" and never learned that it was possible to be very, very injured.

As I watched them travel safely through their three-dimensional maze, I noticed a girl balancing precariously on a single rope. She was around my age, but unlike the other villagers, the scowl on her face told me that she was not happy to see us.

I would not have noticed her at all if it hadn't been for the small reflection of light bouncing off of something at her ankle. The rest of her body was concealed by shadows from the vines, blending in with her surroundings like a gecko on a leaf.

My attention was pulled back to the group surrounding us as the people parted to let an old man through. Without saying a word, he gestured to Flint and Estes before turning to walk back the way he had come. Flint assured me that I was safe here and that he would find me as soon as he was finished, then both men were gone.

The crowd's excitement died down quickly once Flint and Estes left. All of the people went back to doing their own tasks, except one. Across from me sat a young boy with big brown eyes, watching me like I was his hero.

CHAPTER 4
THE SANCTUARY

Being hundreds of feet beneath the surface of the earth did not cast the underground tunnels into darkness as I had expected. Strategically placed glass, mirrors, and water allowed tiny specks of light to come through from the surface and be multiplied through cracks in the ceiling.

The people here had lanterns that they could use if they were walking around between sunset and sunrise on a new moon, but it sounded like they all went to sleep at sunset. I wondered how many people down here had heightened eyesight and would be able to see in the dark without lanterns.

Ollie led me around the compound, providing an unofficial tour of his village beneath the dirt - or as everyone else called it, The Sanctuary.

Ollie seemed to know everybody's business. He introduced me to every person we passed; sometimes asking them very personal questions in a way that is only acceptable for young children to do.

I supposed that's what happened when such a small group of people are together all day long, every single day. Though that never happened at Hope Street, so maybe you had to actually like the people around you.

As we wove through the halls of The Sanctuary, Ollie continued to make observations about my appearance. I caught him eyeing the red hat strapped to my backpack like it was a ruby.

He asked questions about everything from my clothing to my haircut. I had entered a strange new world, but to him, I was the stranger.

His clothing was dyed with pigments from the earth and made of natural fibers; probably the vines that grew all around us, while my shirt had a brightly colored design on the front. Although some of the other inhabitants wore jeans, they were so worn that they made my dusty jeans look brand new. I wondered how often people came and went. Surely they sent people out for supplies, right?

Ollie explained their market system to me. Everybody had a role that was unique to their skills. If they needed help with something, they asked the person with the skill set most fitted to the job.

They kept all of their tools in one area, and all of the extra fabric in another area. If you needed to use it, you just borrowed it and put it back when you were done. Ollie said that there was even an area where he put his outgrown clothes and was able to get a bigger size as he went through growth spurts.

The food was stored in the kitchen area, which was next to the cavern housing the farm and chickens. I was very curious what an underground farm looked like, but Ollie just pointed in the general direction of the farm as we walked past that area.

As he gave me a tour, Ollie took the opportunity to tell me about life in The Sanctuary. He was born down here and didn't know any other way to live. Everything he knew about the "top-side" was what he learned from novels and magazines that had been brought to The Sanctuary.

Ollie was eager for me to provide him with an updated first-hand account of the top-side. I was eager to learn more about The Sanctuary and all of the Heightened people who lived in it. In this way, he was the perfect person to be my tour guide. Our lives were so similar, yet so very, very different.

There was a price to pay for keeping The Sanctuary a secret. Ollie was not ignorant to the outside world, my world, by choice. He and the other inhabitants lived by strict rules about where they were allowed to go, and what they were allowed to do if they went there. The village elders forbade their people from entering the outside world.

There were only two exceptions.

The first exception allowed a small group to conduct brief training exercises within a short distance of the entrance. This kept them far away from civilization, while still being able to practice real world scenarios. I wasn't sure how the middle of the desert helped them prepare for the real world full of huge cities and people, but I kept those thoughts to myself.

The second exception was for three people who had permission to journey wherever they felt necessary, to ensure the safety of the Heightened. Flint and Estes were on this list.

Ollie was not on either list.

As a guest of The Sanctuary, I had to follow their rules. I knew that Flint would let me decide if and when we left, but according to Ollie, if somebody without clearance left The Sanctuary, they risked being caught and interrogated or tortured by Stratus.

I felt a twang of sadness for him, that he grew up worrying about being interrogated and tortured if he went outside. There was a guilty pit in my stomach as I remembered that I had used that word more than once to describe what happened at Hope Street.

As we continued walking, I noted that each room was very different from the last; each having their own unique function. I caught a brief glimpse into some of their training rooms. Small rock pillars were spread across the floor of one room, while another room was entirely empty except for the ropes hanging from the ceiling. Nobody was in the training rooms as we walked past, but I hoped to see them in use at some point. Until then, I would have to use my imagination.

The Sanctuary provided safety, but there was an underlying expectation of danger which resulted in constant training and skill mastery. When I asked Ollie about it, he said that he had been taught his entire life to "prepare for the worst and hope for the best."

Children in The Sanctuary went through a rite of passage called the "Epic Descent" on the night before their thirteenth birthday. This consisted of the twelve year old climbing to the top of the highest cavern, and jumping off to land in the deep water below. The next day, they were allowed to join the top side training class.

All undescended training classes, like the one Ollie was assigned to, were limited to the training rooms.

Ollie smiled from ear to ear as he informed me that he was only a few years away from his Epic Descent. His excitement was infectious and I couldn't help but smile back.

I should have been overwhelmed that my entire existence had shifted; everything I thought I knew about myself and my place in the world was wrong. Instead, I felt relaxed for the first time I could remember. I felt like I was finally at home.

Between his meetings, Flint tracked us down to bring me water and to make sure we were staying out of trouble. He asked if I would like to attend one of the training classes, but Ollie answered before I could even open my mouth.

"That would be so cool! He would love that. I can't wait for him to meet Jax. Jax is the best! Did you know that he holds the record on the ropes course?"

Flint smiled at me and interrupted Ollie before he could continue the story.

"I'll leave you to it then. Don't forget about dinner."

Ollie paused long enough to say goodbye, then picked up right where he left off, giving me a detailed description of how Jax had done it. I remembered all of the times I had been ridiculed, hit, or left out while I was at Hope Street. If Jax and the other kids in my training class were at least half as friendly as Ollie, it would be a huge improvement.

As we made our way towards the dining area, I caught various bits of conversation.

"Thank you so much for your help with the potatoes."

"I would love to try your new loom."

"Her leg should heal soon. I am going to bring her dinner tonight."

"I should have some free time tomorrow if you'd like some help."

It was so different from Hope Street that I felt like I had fallen through a portal into another reality; though I suppose that's exactly what happened, if you switch 'portal' with 'long tunnel.' Everyone was just so *helpful*.

The dining hall consisted of six large rectangular tables that were etched from the earth. Each one was meticulously crafted from a single piece of stone. Ollie caught me gaping at the tables and told me that the stone was called ammolite, and it could be found on most of the inner walls of The Sanctuary.

I realized that the hard, glass-like walls of the entrance must be made out of the same stuff, though I didn't notice any colors in those walls. Maybe it was the way the sun snuck through cracks, because these tables and benches had bright swirls of every color imaginable. It was mesmerizing.

It must have taken years to carve out the six giant ammolite tables and enough benches for these people to fit comfortably. There were several empty seats, and I wondered how often new people joined them. Would the empty spaces fill up eventually as they brought more people like me down here, or were those spaces created for people who had since died? I decided I didn't want to know.

The food was placed on a long platform that sat between the kitchen and the dining area. I stood in front of it for a heartbeat wondering who was going to give me my portion, when I noticed that people were serving themselves. They took as much or as little as they needed before turning to find a place at the tables.

Giddy with the freedom to choose my own food, I helped myself to a large scoop of stew, two small rolls, and a sweet potato. I left the mystery items for another time, though Ollie filled his entire plate with them.

"Come on," Ollie said to me, tilting his head towards the tables. I followed him to one of the benches and set my plate on the table. Suddenly realizing how hungry I was, I devoured my food without saying a single word. When I looked up, Ollie was staring at me.

"You can have more if you want. Once everybody sits down, we are allowed to get more food."

I didn't have it in me to be embarrassed. After living off of pre-packaged food and gas station snacks for nearly three weeks, my stomach was desperate for a fresh meal.

One table sat in front of the rest. It was identical to the other five tables in size and shape, but it had been placed on a small platform and sat across the front of the others so that its occupants seemed to be looking down at us as we ate.

"It's for the Elders," Ollie explained, "they make all the rules."

The leader, Barton, sat in the middle of the table. He was a very tall man, with close-cropped white hair. He seemed like he might be sick, pulling out a blue handkerchief every few minutes to cover his mouth as he coughed. I didn't ask Ollie about that, in case it was a side effect of a more serious disease.

Barton's cane was made entirely of wood. The handle had been carved into the head of a hawk, which seemed to stare at us from on top of the table where it rested.

As I watched, Estes walked up to the table and took the seat next to Barton.

"Estes?" Shocked, I asked Ollie.

"Didn't he tell you? Estes is our Justice. He helps us solve conflicts between people. The Elders all vote when they make big decisions, but the rest of them usually vote the way Estes does." Ollie went on to give me a detailed explanation of all the reasons that he would make an excellent Justice someday.

As I was finishing up my second plate of stew and rolls, I saw Flint walk through the dining room. I waved, but he must not have seen me as he walked up to the Elder's table. I wondered if he was also an Elder, but he stopped in front of the table and spoke to them.

Flint had his back to the rest of the dining hall, so I had to guess what was happening based on his hand gestures and the reaction from the Elders. They didn't seem very interested in what he was saying. When his hands stopped moving and it appeared that he was finished speaking, all of the Elders turned towards Estes for advice. Estes spoke a few words to the rest of the Elders and then turned back towards Flint. One by one, the Elders raised their fists, each with their thumb facing down.

Without saying another word, Flint turned his back to the table and stormed through the dining hall, exiting through one of the tunnels in the back. I stood to go after him, but Ollie grabbed my arm and introduced me to another person.

Once I was able to break away from Ollie, I went looking for Flint and found him sitting alone. I sat next to him on another beautifully carved bench.

"Is everything okay," I asked, knowing I might not get an honest answer out of him.

Flint snorted, but didn't respond for several minutes, using the time to take in bursts of air and let them out in a huff. His mouth opened and closed, as if he were searching for the appropriate response.

"I knew this was coming," he responded. We had been sitting in silence long enough that his voice surprised me.

"What was coming?" I was almost certain I didn't want to know what was so important to him that he had approached the Elders on our first night here, though I couldn't help myself from asking.

Placing his head in his hands, he let out one last sigh before answering.

"I had to make a," he seemed to search for the right words before continuing, "request to the Elders. To search for Stratus, to... put an end to our hiding. This is not a sanctuary; it is a survival bunker. We have survived for so long because we were able to remain hidden, but that's all we do down here; *survive*."

He waved his hand to indicate our surroundings before dropping his voice and leaning his head back against the wall. "This is not living. We have to take our lives back. Looking for Stratus, seeking him out, would put my entire team in danger. I understand that, but they don't seem to understand that every one of us is in danger down here. They seem to have forgotten the resources that Stratus has in his arsenal. He will find this place eventually, and when he does, it will be the end of us all."

I wanted more details, but Flint let out another big huff of air and stood, effectively ending our conversation. Life was a lot simpler before he arrived at Hope Street, back when I could hope for a better, safer life with a loving family. Maybe a dog.

Just seconds after Flint walked away, Ollie filled his vacant spot. He must have been listening and waiting until he could approach me.

"Want me to show you where to sleep," he asked quietly.

I nodded, and we walked in silence through the barely lit corridors until he gestured to a narrow opening in the wall.

The sparse decorations made the enormous room seem even more massive. A handful of hammocks were in one corner near a small fire pit, and the rest of the room was almost entirely empty.

"Who else sleeps in here?" My voice echoed as I peeked curiously at the hammocks.

"This is Estes's room," said Ollie. "Flint usually stays in this room when he's down here. I figured you would want to be with them."

Not knowing when Estes or Flint would be back, Ollie helped me settle into the lowest hammock. He said he wanted me to have a short fall if I rolled out of the hammock in the middle of the night.

He pulled a lever on his way to the door, and a small silver square on the ceiling opened up. It appeared to be part of their strange ventilation system.

"Hey Ollie?" I said it loudly, forgetting that my voice would echo in the chamber. He looked up, waiting for the sound to settle before turning back to me.

"Yeah?"

"I really appreciate everything you did for me today. You know, introducing me to everybody, and showing me around, and helping with the hammock, and just… being nice, I guess."

"You're welcome," he said with a tired smile.

"Do you think," I trailed off, afraid to voice my questions about Flint where so many would be able to hear me.

"Estes probably had a good reason." He shrugged, then he was gone.

CHAPTER 5
BACK TO SCHOOL

Ollie arrived the next morning to walk me to my classes. I couldn't use the sun as a guide to tell me roughly what time it was, but knew it had to be very early because there was barely a sliver of light coming through the cracks in the ceiling.

Excited to join the other teenagers in the training rooms, I launched myself out of bed. As my face hit the floor, I remembered Ollie's worry about me falling from the hammock. Ollie laughed as he tried to help me up.

"Good call on having me use the lowest one," I said as I put my shoes on.

When I turned to say goodbye to Flint and Estesl I realized that they weren't in the room. I didn't hear them come in last night or leave this morning, and I wondered whether they slept somewhere else or were exceptionally good at tiptoeing. For once, the night had been quiet. It felt like I had slept with earplugs in, under a set of soundproof headphones, wrapped in a thick cotton scarf.

Ollie was telling another story about how great Jax was, but all I could think about was Flint's argument with the Elders. I didn't understand how Flint would think that a handful of people, even Heightened people, would be able to win a fight against an entire government organization whose primary function is to kill them. Kill *us*.

Even if Flint was able to convince everybody in the entire Sanctuary to join the fight, how would that be enough to take down an army? I hoped that Flint and Estes had made up after Estes and the rest of the Elders had turned Flint down.

Curious if they would be able to speak privately while surrounded by Heightened, I asked Ollie if there was any place within The Sanctuary where people could have personal conversations. My voice had practically shouted as it echoed the night before, and there had to be some method for having conversations without the entire population hearing you.

"That's easy, there are sound-holders all over the place."

At my confused look, he explained "little rooms that hold in the sound."

"What do you mean, like they're soundproof?" I couldn't understand how any place could be soundproof when they didn't have doors.

As we turned a corner, he pointed to a small alcove that almost looked like they had started to dig a tunnel and then changed their minds. I stepped into it and looked up to find a perfectly domed ceiling.

Ollie pulled me back into the hallway before stepping inside himself.

"Hello," he said while facing me. I could hear him perfectly and debated telling him that the tiny room was, in fact, not soundproof at all. Then he turned to the side.

"Hello," I saw his mouth move but could barely hear him. He turned his back to me and stood there in silence for a few seconds before turning back around and joining me in the hallway, continuing towards the training room.

"Did you hear me when I was facing the other way?"

"No, I didn't hear anything!" I couldn't believe how effective those tiny rooms were. With heightened hearing, I probably would have been able to hear him when he faced the other direction, but I would have had to really focus.

Ollie led me into a large, dark room. He took a few steps in, then stopped and motioned for me to go ahead of him.

"This is for level five people. I'm only a level two, so I can't use this room yet." Ollie explained, still motioning for me to go.

I stopped and walked back to where he stood.

"Why am *I* here?" I tried to walk back into the hallway, but Ollie blocked me.

"Flint wanted you in this one today, so go! Jax gets mad when he has to wait." Ollie said impatiently. I wished Flint was here so I could argue with him directly. After all, it wasn't Ollie's fault that somebody with absolutely no experience was placed three levels above him.

Realizing that I wasn't going to argue with him any longer, he wished me luck and pushed me towards the crowd.

I approached a dozen people who stood at the edge of a large hole in the ground. Most looked like teenagers, but some appeared to be in their early twenties. I turned back to see Ollie happily sitting near the door. He may not have been participating in this class, but he had no problem making himself comfortable while he watched us.

As I got closer, I saw that the hole was actually a large pond. I hoped Flint didn't expect me to finish my Epic Descent on the first day here, and looked up to confirm that nobody was standing on the uppermost platform.

Everyone stood staring into the dark abyss, occasionally muttering to each other about the time. It took my eyes a few minutes to adjust before I was able to see what everyone else could clearly see.

Three people sat at the bottom of the pond, not moving until they uncrossed their legs to swim to the surface. It had been almost twenty minutes, when the last man slowly made his way to the top. Judging by everybody's adoring looks, I assumed that the man was our instructor, Jax.

A few of the remaining students were still trickling in as the instructor dried off. I stood at the edge of the water, looking into the crater and worrying about the tasks they might expect me to complete.

The water was crystal clear and somehow had tiny bits of light reflecting throughout the walls. I didn't see them until my eyes had adjusted, but now I could see straight to the bottom. While I was examining the tiny pieces of light, I noticed a familiar piece of jewelry on the wet foot of the person next to me.

I told myself that she had been scowling at something else as I mustered the confidence to introduce myself to her.

She gave me a withering look and walked away, her black hair leaving a trail of water in her wake.

Nope. I was right the first time. She hated me.

"Everyone in the water," Jax ordered as I stared after her.

Everybody followed his command by immediately jumping into the lake, including me.

"Today we will practice staying calm in a stressful situation. One of the best ways to understand this is to complete this lesson under water. The more anxious you become, the more energy you deplete, the more air you use. On the top side, this is the difference between life and death." He looked at us meaningfully.

I couldn't keep the fear from showing on my face as I kicked hard to keep my head above water.

"Let's see what you can do. On my mark, I want everyone to the bottom. Take a deep breath, and three…two…one."

Everybody flipped upside down and swam straight to the bottom, where Jax and the grumpy girl had been sitting when I first entered the room.

I don't know how long my first attempt lasted. It felt like a lifetime, though I was the last person to reach the bottom and had to immediately swim back to the surface. I had plenty of time to catch my breath as I swam to the side of the pond and held onto the rock, allowing my body to rest.

I watched in amazement as the other students sat motionless beneath me for at least five minutes before they started swimming to the surface. The last person was able to hold their breath for almost ten minutes.

By the end of class, I was able to stay underwater for three minutes. Those three minutes consisted of me calmly holding my breath for one minute and spending the next two minutes thrashing around in an attempt to stay underwater.

Though the other students were still much better than me, I was proud of my growth until I saw the girl with the anklet smirking coldly at me. I had tried my best, but I could not compete with people who had been doing this for their entire lives.

Jax whistled to get our attention.

"Last exercise of the day. Everybody grab a challenge box."

There was a pile of small wooden boxes on the ledge of the water, each box containing a different puzzle. Our assignment was to bring our box to the bottom of the pond and solve the puzzle before swimming back up.

I was barely able to reach the bottom; I wouldn't have time to play a game while I was down there.

"This should be fun," I muttered under my breath, forgetting my company. Every head in the room turned my way before their focus shifted back to their own wooden boxes. Embarrassed, I realized that I would need to acclimate to being around people who could hear a whisper as easily as a shout.

Still recovering from my previous attempt, I grabbed my box and waited for Jax to count down again. At his command, I took a deep breath and swam down. When I reached the bottom, I opened my puzzle box and immediately lost one of the pieces in a crevice between two rocks. I squeezed my hand into the crack and could barely touch it with my finger, but did not have enough space to get a finger underneath the piece to pick it up.

I frantically swam around the bottom of the lake looking for a tool to use, turning over rocks and wiggling my hand into cracks. I finally found a thin piece of metal about the size of a credit card, and used it to nudge the puzzle piece out from under the rock. With it, I was able to put half of the puzzle together before my body begged me to take another breath. I left the box and unassembled pieces there and swam to the top as quickly as I was able.

I gagged and coughed as I clutched the safety of the surface rocks. When I had recovered enough energy to pull my exhausted body from the water, I flopped onto the rocky floor. Eyes closed, I reminded myself that everybody in the room could hear a pin drop and attempted to gasp for air as quietly as possible.

When I was confident that I wouldn't lose consciousness, I sat up and opened my eyes.

Everybody was staring at me. They must have finished their puzzles and come to the top while I was laying on the side.

I pulled my knees to my chest and turned away from them, trying to hide the humiliation on my face.

"How did you do that?" One of the other students asked.

When nobody responded, I turned to face them. They were still looking at me, and Ollie was with them.

His brown eyes were huge in his face.

"Do you know how long you were down there?" He asked.

Not wanting to hurt Ollie's feelings, I tried to shut down the topic without being mean.

"One of my pieces fell in a crack, so, I mean, I had to get it, and,"

"Forty minutes!" Ollie interrupted, beaming with excitement. "That's longer than I have seen *anyone* hold their breath! Ever!"

I thought maybe they were just being mean to the new kid, but Ollie wasn't the type of person to do that to somebody.

I realized that everybody else in the room looked shocked, unsettled, or - in the case of the grumpy girl - grumpy. All except Ollie, who looked like he was holding in a million questions for me.

Even Jax looked confused as he excused our class for the day and walked towards the hallway. Without turning his head, Jax grumbled, "don't forget the box."

I slid into the water as smoothly as possible, trying to avoid a splash which might draw attention. As if there was anybody in the room not already staring at me. I swam to the bottom, grabbed the box and puzzle pieces, and came straight back to the top.

As I dried off, I realized I had a lingering spectator. It was the girl with the anklet. Her hair had dried, though there was still a puddle under her feet.

She still looked unfriendly, but it was much less threatening than the look she had given me the day before. Maybe she was warming up to me. I gave her a small smile, but she just turned and left the room.

Maybe she *wasn't* warming up to me.

Ollie put all of the puzzles together as he waited for me to finish changing into dry clothes.

I dried off using one of their homemade towels, which was surprisingly absorbent, then put on my jeans and a new fibrous shirt Ollie had brought me. I needed to figure out how they wash their laundry, but first I needed to know who my enemies were.

"When we first got here, there was a girl in the water with Jax. Did you see her?"

"Sam?" He looked confused.

"Does Sam have black hair," I asked tentatively, wondering why he was giving me that look.

"Yeah, that's Sam. She's my sister. I wanted to introduce you, but she must have been in a hurry because she left so quickly. I guess she will have to meet you later. Actually, I was going to introduce you yesterday, but I couldn't find her anywhere! It was so funny because she's usually so bossy and I can't get away from her, but then yesterday it was like she disappeared! Do you have a crush on her? It's okay if you do."

He laughed before he started peppering me with all of his questions about my special technique for holding breath, and I made a mental note to stay far away from whatever area Ollie and his family called home.

CHAPTER 6
SQUIBITS AND PUPILS

I sat next to Flint as we roasted squibits over the small fire in our room. The small brown vegetables were the only dessert option available. As they cooked, their color changed to dark purple, which meant they were ready to be eaten. Although they were unappealing to look at, they were delicious.

I was roasting my ninth squibit when Estes greeted us. I had almost forgotten that we were in his room.

"'ello," I attempted with a full mouth. I waved at him with a sticky hand and continued roasting my current squibit.

Flint had the opposite reaction, attempting to ignore Estes in the most nonchalant way possible, by acting like he hadn't noticed Estes was there. I hadn't seen them in the same room together since the event in the cafeteria the day before, and I wondered if this was the first time they were seeing each other.

Flint hadn't brought up the topic with me again, but he had been moody all afternoon. It wasn't hard to figure out what was bothering him. Estes attempted small talk, but Flint only gave him one-word responses. The tension was so thick, I considered abandoning my roasting squibit and wandering around The Sanctuary alone.

I was relieved when the two of them finally stepped into a small domed closet at the opposite side of the room. Now that I knew what the rooms were, I noticed them all over The Sanctuary.

I wondered if all of the Elders had one inside their room, or if Estes was special for having his own private sound-holder.

They talked for quite a while, but I was content just sitting there. My belly was full of sugary squibits, my body was warm from the fire, and my muscles were tired from the training.

I hadn't realized my eyes were closed until I heard angry stomping feet and looked up to find Estes storming out of his room while Flint walked back to me and sat in a huff.

"Everything okay?" I asked hesitantly.

"Just a little chat between old friends." Flint said it calmly, but his furrowed brows and clenched jaw told me that he definitely had not seen it as a "chat."

He speared squibits onto his stick so aggressively that I found myself relieved when he finished and held the stick over the fire without accidentally impaling his hand.

We sat in silence for a few minutes while I listened to his breathing settle down.

Flint eventually spoke. "I heard about the dive today."

"I'm not really sure what happened." I responded.

"You know, your dad was the only other person who could hold their breath like that. I see a lot of him in you." Flint said. He was staring into the fire as he said it, but I got the feeling that he was watching me out of the corner of his eyes.

I didn't have any other part of them; no memories, no mementos, only the fact that these people told me I looked like my parents, and whatever heightened abilities I had acquired from them. I wished I had more, but I would take whatever small pieces of them I could get.

"Can you introduce me to the person who has pictures of my parents? I mean, if they're down here."

"Hmm? Oh, yes, tomorrow I'll bring you over there."

I couldn't help myself as hope bloomed in my chest.

"I won't be able to dive like him again." I didn't want Flint expecting me to do the impossible.

"Be patient. You have only skimmed the surface of what you can do," he said seriously, then snorted and added, "maybe not the surface, maybe you swam to the bottom of what you can do."

Uncomfortable with his sudden mood shift, I laughed awkwardly before falling back into silence.

His squibits had darkened and turned purple before I spoke.

"If I try really hard, sometimes I can hear things, but I still can't do most of the things you do. Everybody down here is better than me at," I paused, thinking of all the things I had seen since arriving, "at everything, I guess. The only thing I am good at is holding my breath, and I don't even know how I did that."

I felt like I was a disappointment to the memory of my parents.

Flint scoffed.

"Those things are just a small part of being Heightened. None of us have exactly the same abilities. We all have an area that we excel at, but even so, some of us have stronger abilities. Those of us with the strongest abilities become Elders.

"There are legends of Heightened who could see into the future or move things with their minds. Maybe they are just fairy tales, maybe not. Even so, ability is nothing without effort. You have worked harder to hone your abilities in the past few weeks than most of us. Once we identify your talents, I have no doubt that you will learn to harness them."

While I was flattered at his faith in me, I couldn't help but wonder what made him think I should be in a level five class.

"Why was I in that water class today? Ollie said it was only for advanced students, and I didn't even know what 'Heightened' meant until a few weeks ago."

"I apologize if that was uncomfortable for you, but we don't have the luxury of time. You need to ride this bicycle without training wheels."

Ollie plopped down next to me and jumped right into the conversation.

"Have you ever been on a real bicycle? That was so cool today! How did you hold your breath that long? I've never seen anybody do it that long. Everyone is talking about you."

Flint took advantage of the diversion.

"Don't stay up too late," he warned, though there was humor in his eyes. He handed his stick of perfectly-cooked squibits to Ollie and dismissed himself.

Still feeling overwhelmed from the training and my worry about whatever was happening between Flint and Estes, I quickly moved to a different subject to avoid Ollie's interrogation. It was almost too easy to divert his attention to the topic of his hero, Jax.

I was curious about the instructor. He couldn't have been more than twenty years old, but he was easily the most beloved person in the Sanctuary. I was rewarded for my effort; Ollie could have written a book about Jax.

Ollie explained every detail of Jax's life, from him being brought to The Sanctuary as a little boy, to earning the title of 'instructor' at only seventeen. Ollie recounted every time Jax had spoken to him. If it were possible, I am sure Ollie would have had a poster of Jax hanging above his bed, er, hammock.

A steppingstone to Jax's fame within The Sanctuary was something called the Trials. It was a two-day event that took place every summer. Everybody was allowed to compete in the tests on mental acuity, athletic ability, and physical strength. Everybody found a way to be part of the event; either by setting it up, keeping score, or participating.

Jax had won the last three Trials and, according to Ollie, was favored to win the next one.

Ollie and I had been talking for so long that the fire had almost run out of fuel. He turned away from me, picking up two smaller logs from the pile of chopped wood. When he turned back to the fire, I fell sideways in my rush to get away from him.

Ollie practically threw his small logs across the room as he rushed to help me up, but I could not hide my shock at his change in appearance. The pupils of his eyes had doubled in size, completely covering his irises. He looked like something out of a horror movie.

I scrambled to my feet, but by that time his eyes had returned to normal.

"What is," he began to say, at the same time that I stammered "Your…"

We both grew silent. Him waiting for me to tell him what was wrong, and me searching for a way to explain his eyes without using the term 'demon'.

"My what?" Said Ollie with a straight face as if not knowing what just happened to him.

"Your eye, er… eyes."

"My *eyes*?" Ollie screeched while nervously touching his fingers to his face.

"They were black. Like, the pupils are all…" I said shakily.

Ollie stared at me for a second before his hands fell from his face, then he spoke to me like I was a scared puppy. "Big? Are my pupils big?"

I deflated. "It's normal for us, isn't it?"

"It. Is. Dark." Ollie replied slowly, emphasizing each word.

The pieces clicked together in my brain. I had been so focused on my own training that I completely overlooked a skill that everybody else seemed to have; dilating their pupils on demand.

This also explained how Estes and Flint were able to smoothly walk down the dark tunnel when we first arrived, while I had to stumble behind them with a lantern.

I was embarrassed that I was probably the only person in the Sanctuary who didn't know how to do this.

"Could you," I began to ask, before he interrupted with an offer to teach me.

I sat patiently across from him as he put out every last bit of the fire. Once the light had gone out and the room was enveloped in darkness, he began giving me instructions.

I attempted to enlarge my pupils as Ollie described, straining my eyes as if focusing on something far away. I started to see the outline of Ollie's face a few times, but I could not maintain my focus.

After a few minutes, I physically could not do it any longer. My eyes ached to the point that I found it unbearable to keep them open without excruciating pain. With my eyes clenched shut, I allowed Ollie to guide me back to my hammock.

I listened to Ollie's optimistic voice tell me that I would be better once my eye muscles grew stronger. He said most toddlers in the Sanctuary take months to learn, but that he was sure I would be able to dilate my pupils faster than that.

Comparing me to a toddler didn't comfort me the way he thought it would.

The overwhelming ache behind my eyes depleted my energy and left me with no desire to try again. Ever. The only thing I wanted at that moment was to go to sleep for a very long time.

"How long will it take to stop hurting?" I asked Ollie with my eyes still shut.

"You should feel fine when you wake up tomorrow morning," Ollie responded as he got me situated in my hammock. The last thing I wanted was to fall out of it. Again.

I thought Ollie would leave the room once I was safely balanced inside my hammock, but instead I could hear him fiddling around with the fire. Shortly after that, I heard Flint join him. As the pounding inside my head receded, I thought about joining them, but quickly changed my mind when I attempted to open my eyes. It would be best to stay where I was.

CHAPTER 7
THE END OF THE ROPE

Ollie and I were already walking to my training room by the time the morning light made its way down to the Sanctuary. The halls in the main areas had become familiar enough that I didn't need too much help from Ollie, though I did stumble quite a few times in the dark.

As always, other people greeted us as we crossed paths. I was excited to realize that most of them looked familiar to me now, and that I was able to remember some of their names.

We passed a boy who seemed to be about Ollie's age. The boy was walking with his mother and I realized that I had never met Ollie's parents. He almost always sat with me when we ate, and he never invited me to his room at night. I wondered if they were at The Sanctuary, or if they were out tracking lost kids like what Flint did with me.

"Do you have any other siblings besides Sam?" I turned to wave to a group headed in the opposite direction before turning back to Ollie.

"Well, you probably noticed that there aren't very many kids down here. Not like what you're used to, I'm sure. Sam is the only one that I am related to by blood, but when you spend time with the same twenty kids your whole life, it feels like all of them are your siblings. I don't know if that makes sense to *you*."

He said "you" like I had grown up on a different planet. I guess, compared to the way Ollie was raised at The Sanctuary, growing up with other kids *was* an alien experience.

"What about your parents? What are they like? I don't think I met them yet." I hoped he had a good relationship with them. It was hard to listen to people complain about their parents when I wanted my own back so badly.

For the first time since I met Ollie, his carefree smile faded away as he glanced towards the floor.

"They died when I was little," Ollie answered. "I barely remember them."

"I am so sorry Ollie," I said as my heart sunk.

I was sorry. Sorry for him, sorry for me, sorry for Sam even though she hated me.

"It's okay." He gave me a small smile and lifted one shoulder as if to shrug it off. "It was a long time ago and I don't really remember much. Most of what I know is what other people have told me. Everybody said that my family was crossing the street, and a car came towards us. I guess it was going too fast for us to get out of the way, so Dad only had time to push Sam off the road. Mom was holding me, but somehow I was ok even though she wasn't. Afterwards, they brought Sam and me here, and now I have lots of moms, especially Sam. She's really bossy." He rolled his eyes and began to smile before his face fell again. "Nobody ever found the driver."

I wanted to tell him that I understood, that I knew what it was like to want the things that other kids took for granted; to have somebody to tuck you in at night and give advice and even somebody to send you to your room when you messed up. I opened my mouth to say so, but found myself thinking about his parents' death.

Everybody down here had special skills. Hearing. Vision. Speed.

Cars were *loud*.

How did a car sneak up on two Heightened? They didn't see or hear the car until it was too late to use their super speed and get out of the way? It didn't make sense.

"Are you ready?"

I looked at Ollie, confused, until I heard a light chatter coming from the training room. I didn't know if I'd ever be ready for what happened in there, but I couldn't say that, so I just smiled encouragingly.

I felt immediate relief to see that this training room didn't have any open water trenches. The space appeared to be completely vacant, much like Estes's room. Ollie and I walked towards the group of students gathered at the far end of the room and I remembered the training room I had seen on my first day here. Nervously, I looked up.

Jax was climbing one of the ropes that hung from the thirty-foot ceiling. Each rope was a different length and thicknesses, and two of them had been dyed a dark reddish color. A few clusters of ceiling hooks were empty, exposing the natural rock of the cavern.

Jax explained that the exercise would be for us to pair off and race each other up the red ropes. Once we reached the top, we were to use the ropes to swing to the other side of the room and back, then ring the bell above. The winner was, obviously, the person who rang the bell first.

This exercise reminded me of racing against Dillon during P.E. class, but I would fall thirty feet this time instead of three. There were no harnesses to catch us at the top, and no nets to catch us at the bottom. Even the other students seemed nervous about this exercise, and they had been swinging from ropes since they were children.

Ollie put his hand on my elbow and whispered that I should probably just watch from the sidelines. I did not need any further convincing.

The most difficult parts of this activity would be finding a way to cross the vacant spots on the ceiling. They would have to swing hard enough to launch their body across the open area, and catch a rope on the other side. While they were swinging on one rope, they would need to instantly calculate the speed and strength needed for their next swing, and then have the finesse to pull it off.

"Everybody line up," Jax shouted at the front of the room. Two by two, the other students started racing one another for the chance to go first. I sat with Ollie and watched from the sidelines, again being reminded of Coach Curtis's P.E. class. The Sanctuary had more similarities to my old life than I expected.

I watched each of the students climb and gracefully swing from one end of the room to the other. None of them dared to cross the third gap, taking extra time to swing around the vacancy, but it still seemed impossible. Once again, I was grateful that Ollie was with me. At least I wasn't sitting on the sidelines alone.

As the last two students finished swinging and came back down, Jax asked the students to form a semicircle around him. His back was to me, but then he turned around and smiled at me. "It looks like our water prodigy wanted to go last." Now I saw his smile for what it was; a challenge. He positioned them like that, all facing me, so they would witness my humiliation.

I tried to sound nonchalant as I responded, "That's okay. I'm just a spectator today," but I was sure the blush creeping up my neck gave me away.

"Don't be ridiculous. This should be easy for you," Jax replied, his smile growing more into a smirk as his comment dripped with insincerity. All at once, I hated him. At least Dillon knew he was a bully. Jax was a bully hiding inside the body of Ollie's hero.

Again, I politely declined, but Jax refused to leave me alone. Making an exaggerated show of looking at all of the students, he announced that each of them had already completed their turn. With a disappointed sigh, he announced that he would have to be my challenge partner, though I was sure he had planned it this way from the beginning. The disappointment was mine alone, but I would not back down to somebody like *him*.

I anxiously made my way to the end of my red rope, grasping it tightly in my sweaty palms. I looked back to see Ollie with his mouth wide open, shaking his head in disapproval. His hands were clenched in fists at his chest, as if he was helping me hold the rope.

We started our ascent quickly. My heart was pounding harder and faster as I climbed further from the floor. The only benefit to being so far off the ground was my hope that the other students couldn't see the sheer panic written across my face. Jax, however, had a front row seat as he glared at me from his red rope. I began to feel lightheaded as my breathing increased, and I hoped I wasn't about to faint.

Jax and I were almost side-by-side when we reached the top of our red ropes, but he quickly took the lead as we made our way across the ceiling. He moved from one rope to the next without a second thought. I, on the other hand, swung back and forth on the first rope, making sure I would be able to catch the next rope before I let go of the one I was currently on.

Jax was already across the second gap in our sequence as I reached the first gap. He was swinging back towards me as if he was toying with me. We both knew there was no chance that I would beat him. I leaped through the air of the first gap, but couldn't get a firm grip on the next rope. My hands flailed through the air as I tried desperately to catch it.

My hands found a grip and I dangled from the bottom of the rope like my life depended on it, which it did, as I tried to catch my breath and reminded myself not to look down.

I should have been too terrified to go on, but instead I felt determined. Adrenaline wiped away the exhaustion in my muscles, and I found myself across the second gap and on my way to the third. The danger was real but I had already gone too far. My only option was to finish.

I was flying across the third gap when all of the fear from my first jump slammed back into my body. As I floated through the air I quickly realized just how far this gap was. I reached for the rope on the other side, but I wasn't close enough. As I fell towards the ground, I very ungracefully flailed my entire body in one last attempt to catch a rope.

I felt the rope catch, and was equal parts relieved and embarrassed. I squeezed my eyes closed, wishing I could disappear. Was that one of my powers?

I opened my eyes to see Ollie, and everyone else, looking up to watch as I dangled from the bottom of a rope. My right wrist had been caught in a knot at the end of the rope. I struggled to untie the knot with my left hand. Without warning, I was released from my confinement.

The landing was rough, but it looked like a bruised wrist would be my only injury. Quite an improvement, since I had been bracing for death a few seconds ago. Rubbing my wrist, I looked up to thank Jax for his small amount of human decency. I was caught by surprise to see Sam making her way down the rope. She was the last person I expected to come to my aid. Besides Jax.

"Thank you." I gave her a hesitant smile.

"You're welcome," she replied with a small smile of her own.

"I don't think we've formally met. I'm Kai." I said, reaching out with my injured hand.

"I know. Your wrist looks pretty bad." She said it kindly as she rotated my wrist instead of shaking my hand.

I looked back at my classmates and found Jax smugly watching my exchange with Sam. As I made eye contact with him, he called across the room, "I am so sorry, I really thought you would be good at that. I guess I was wrong."

Gritting my teeth, I turned away to him.

Worse. Than. Dillon.

"It will be fine. Just a bruise, see?" I tried to ignore the pain as I gently rotated my wrist.

"Well, a bruise can become serious. I'll bring you to the infirmary to get it checked out". She turned and started walking away, and I hurried to follow.

We made our way out of the room while Jax began the next lesson as if nothing had happened. Ollie walked out with us, but had to attend his own training classes. Before leaving, he asked if he could come by Estes's room later that night to check on me. It was really nice to have somebody who wanted to check on me.

It was still surprising to see how large The Sanctuary really was. Halls and corridors went for miles in all directions. I had familiarized myself with every inch of my world at Hope Street, but that was only a fraction of the size of The Sanctuary. I wondered if I would ever have this place fully memorized the way I did with Hope Street.

"I'm sorry about the other day." Sam said, breaking the silence. "Top siders make me nervous, and we don't get many strangers down here."

"It's fine," I responded; happy her hatred wasn't personal, yet still a little suspicious that she would lead me to a dark tunnel and leave me, knowing I would never find my way back.

"So, you lived on the top side your whole life?" Sam asked, changing the subject.

"Until the day I came here." I nodded, but kept an eye on where we were going so I would be able to find my way back.

"Have you ever seen a Garibaldi?" She asked. I wasn't sure where this conversation was going, and I was about to make a sarcastic comment about her sudden change in topic, but then I looked over at her face.

"Do you mean the fish?" I asked sincerely. The eagerness in her eyes reminded me so much of Ollie that I couldn't bear to tease her about it.

"Yes, of course. Have you? In real life?" She asked again.

Rubbing the back of my head with my uninjured hand, I felt embarrassed that I hadn't seen one. I hadn't seen much of anything. My trip to The Sanctuary with Flint was more exciting than everything else I had experienced in my entire life, combined. Once again failing an attempt to sound nonchalant, I replied, "I have never seen a garibaldi."

Sam reached into her back pocket and pulled out a crumpled magazine with a picture of a whale sprawled across the cover. She quickly flipped to a page featuring an article on the big golden fish. From the condition of the magazine and how quickly she turned to the page, it was obvious that she had read through it a few hundred times. She talked about marine life the way normal people talk about other planets, which made sense for somebody who had never seen either in real life. This worn out magazine was the closest she had ever been to the ocean, much like the Hope Street rooftop was the closest I would ever be to Cassiopeia. I told her about the flowing reddish-blue betta fish in the warden's office back at Hope Street. It lived alone, since it fought any other fish he put in the bowl. I had no interest in the fish then and didn't even give it a second look when I was there, but Sam reacted like I had seen a dinosaur.

I pointed with my good hand to a small patch of Ammolite that was on a nearby wall and told her the scales of the fish resembled tiny flakes of it. She immediately went over and examined it as if she was looking at the fish itself, gently wiping her hands across the wall as if she had never seen the Ammolite before.

Any awkwardness between us disappeared as she prodded me with question after question regarding my experiences with fish. I laughed as she wondered why anybody would go swimming in the ocean when there were killer whales and sharks waiting to eat them. I was so absorbed in our conversation that I had forgotten the pain. When we arrived at the two large double-doors that led to infirmary, the distractions disappeared and the pain came flooding back.

She became serious as she pointed towards the handle.

"This is you," she said before turning to walk back down the hall we had just come from.

I looked after her one last time. Her hair swayed back and forth like a metronome. She turned a corner and was gone from my view. Using my left hand, I fumbled with the handle and managed to swing the heavy door open.

As soon as I let go, the door began to close again. I rushed inside in an attempt to avoid being crushed, and slammed into one of the doctor's assistants. He must have come to investigate when he heard me fumbling around in the hallway.

Squinting his eyes, he scrutinized my face. Finally resigned to the fact that I was a stranger, he quickly sanitized a cut on my elbow that I hadn't noticed, and helped me put a brace on my wrist.

"Wear this until it feels better." He said without any sympathy while gently but forcefully leading me out the door.

I spun around to thank him, but the door was already closed. Realizing that he never introduced himself or asked me who I was, I wondered if news of my arrival had already spread to everybody in The Sanctuary. Maybe that was what happened when you know everything about every other person.

I cradled my wrist gently against my chest as I walked back to Estes's room. It was easy enough to find; I just followed the noise to the dining hall, then went around the side until I found his small doorway.

After changing my clothes and brushing my teeth, I joined everybody else for lunch. Flint had promised to show me the photo of my parents today, but he wasn't in the dining hall. He didn't sleep in Estes's room that night or the next.

CHAPTER 8
THE UP-TOP

Estes made certain I was busy every day. He even went so far as to have Ollie wake me up every morning for my classes. Each week, I had a new assignment to learn on-the-job skills, which I attended after my morning trainings to hone my Heightened abilities. Most mornings, I was awake before Ollie arrived.

The most fascinating part was that I was no longer tired and jittery in the mornings like I had been while I was living at Hope Street. I should have been exhausted by the new workout and training regimen that Estes had me on, but instead I felt stronger and healthier than I had ever felt before.

Ollie crept into Estes's room early each morning, eager to accompany me to class. While we walked through the tunnels, his endless chatter kept me informed of the things I had missed while we were apart. He always sat in the back of my training room, watching us practice until he had to leave for his own classes. Regardless of how far away his class was, he always returned with sweat dripping down his face by the time my class was finished. I knew he had sprinted the entire way. Before I knew it, a month had flown by and I had become accustomed to my new schedule.

I woke up to the excited shrieking of Ollie beside my cot. Words were bursting out of his mouth before I had the chance to open my eyes. He spoke so quickly that I could only decipher a few words. Fortunately, I had grown fluent in Ollie-talk and I was able to connect the dots. It appeared that Ollie was going to be allowed to go outside of The Sanctuary.

"I thought you were still a couple of years away!" I said, surprised and happy for him.

"Special circumstances. Flint is going to bring you to the up-top today and he agreed to take me with you. Can you believe it?" He shrieked while spinning in a circle and pounding his fists up in the air repeatedly.

Flint came into the room. It was the first time I had seen him in several days.

"Is that true, Flint? Are we leaving The Sanctuary?"

"I thought it was time to get started on some outside exercises. Go fill up your pack with food and water for the day. We won't be back until very late." Flint commanded. "Ollie, go get Jax. He's coming too." Flint gave orders in Ollie's general direction.

It didn't take long for Ollie to return with Jax and two filled packs; they were ready to go. Ollie and I followed Flint and Jax like lost puppy dogs through the back corridors. Unlike the parts of The Sanctuary I had grown accustomed to, we walked down dark cobweb-covered tunnels that showed no signs of any recent visitors. Even Ollie didn't know where the tunnels led.

After weaving through the dark and cramped tunnels, we made it to the opening shortly after sunrise.

"Keep your wits about you," Flint said before allowing us to step into the light.

I almost forgot how desolate it was in the up-top, but I didn't care. The sand was beautiful. The air was fresh. It felt as if the sun's warmth had not touched my skin in years. It was amazing, but not as amazing as it felt to watch Ollie experience the outside world for the first time. He stood in silence with his eyes wide open, as he tried to take it all in.

From the corner of my eye, I noticed Flint going through his supplies; double-checking that he had everything he needed. I knew that he didn't truly need to re-check; he was just allowing Ollie to experience the moment before we started walking.

Jax seemed to have the opposite reaction as he stood with a stern and unimpressed look on his face. If there was any hint of enjoyment in him, he hid it well.

"We don't have all day. Let's go!" Jax hollered as he started us on the trek.

After roaming the desert for half of the day while listening to Flint's lectures about outdoor survival, we eventually came to a halt. We were about a hundred feet up on a small overhang with no place to go except the way we had come. Taking this as a sign that we would be turning back, I pulled out my pouch and took a few gulps of water before we started up again. As I looked out on the desert to enjoy my much-needed rest, I realized this wasn't the end of our journey.

Flint was not resting. Instead, he was preparing to move forward. He poked his head over the side of the overhang to gauge the distance down and the correct path for us to take. I waited for Flint to reach into his bag for some rope and carabineers so that we could begin belaying our way down, but he never did.

Instead, Flint called us over to where he was and told us to start our descent. Jax walked over, and without any hesitation, made his way down with ease. Once on the ground, Jax looked back up at the rest of us with a scowl on his face. It was as if he was shocked that we weren't at the bottom with him already.

Ollie went next. He also made his way down with ease, and was standing next to his hero at the bottom. I was amazed at how simple they made it look.

It was my turn, but I couldn't bring myself to take that first step over the edge. We were almost a hundred feet up and I could only think of all the ways this exercise could go wrong. I stood at the top as I waited for the feeling of panic to subside. I looked to Flint for some words of encouragement, but instead found him looking into the distance with a confused look on his face. I began to ask what was wrong but he pressed his hand across my mouth and pulled me to the ground, holding me underneath him. Then he whispered the two words I had been dreading since I met him.

"They're here."

Before I had time to respond, Flint had launched himself over the side of the cliff towards Ollie and Jax. I stood up immediately, and saw three men spring from behind rock pilings to grab Jax and Ollie before Flint even made it to the bottom.

One of the men was dragging Ollie backwards towards his motorcycle, which he had hidden behind some dried brush. It looked like he would succeed in escaping; Ollie swung his arms and kicked his feet, but was unable to break free from the man's firm grip.

Panicking, I raced to the bottom of the cliff. On the way, I saw Flint running after Ollie and his abductor as they prepared to ride away. Ollie's struggle appeared to overwhelm the driver. The motorcycle began to topple side-to-side until the driver lost control, which launched both Ollie and his captor from the crash just as I reached the bottom.

The man quickly recovered from the fall, regaining control of his motorcycle as Flint arrived at Ollie's unmoving body. The man drove straight towards Flint and fired his pistol at us. Before he could take a second shot, Flint grabbed a dagger from his boot and launched it at the man.

The man tried to block the dagger with his arm, but it went through his hand and sent him tumbling to the desert floor.

He stood up hastily, grabbed the knife with his right hand, and tore it from his left hand without any indication of pain. He seemed to realize that Flint's skills exceeded his own, as he gave us one last assessing look before picking up his motorcycle and driving away.

By the time Flint turned his attention away from Ollie, it was too late to save Jax. The other two men had already injected Jax with something that knocked him unconscious. His limp body had been slung over the back of their motorcycle as they made their way across the desert. It was obvious from their perfectly choreographed moves and rugged appearance that they were trained to fight.

The men wore military clothing; desert camouflage pants with beige shirts and combat boots. One man had a scar across his cheek, presumably from a blade. The other man was missing half of his pinky finger. They had matching tattoos on their right biceps, but I wasn't able to get a good look at the design.

Only a cloud of dust was visible as we stared helplessly after them, their motorcycles glinting in the desert sun.

Flint hovered over Ollie, his hand gently touching Ollie's chest to check for broken bones.

"Is he okay?" I whispered hopefully with the last of the air left in my lungs.

"We need to get him back to The Sanctuary. He is breathing, but he may have some internal bleeding. If we aren't back in time, he could die."

I knew Flint was torn between bringing Ollie back to The Sanctuary and following Jax's abductors across the desert. With Ollie's injuries and our lack of resources, the only realistic option was for the three of us to return to The Sanctuary. We had to get Ollie help, tell the others what had happened, and form a search party for Jax.

I just hoped we got back in time.

CHAPTER 9
TIME IS OF THE ESSENCE

The night came too quickly. The temperature dropped a few degrees as soon as the sun dipped below the horizon, and continued to drop with each passing minute. The blinding sun and scorching heat were replaced with twinkling stars and the howling of coyotes. My warm breath came out in white puffs against the cold desert air.

The faint scraping of our makeshift stretcher was the only sound we made. Ollie's body looked even smaller than usual as he lay unmoving on Flint's coat, tied between two large sticks.

It had been hours since Ollie was thrown from the motorcycle, and he still had not moved or opened his eyes. I felt a frequent need to confirm that his chest continued to rise and fall. If nothing else, those small movements gave me a glimmer of hope.

We had only stopped twice since the attack, and even then, only long enough to check Ollie's condition before we continued the long walk back. The initial shock of the ambush was gone, along with my adrenaline, and I was struggling with each step. With my body collapsing, I found it difficult to maneuver around the prickly cacti in the dark. I used Flint as my compass. He traveled around the dark desert terrain the way I once moved around my room back at Hope Street.

We stopped once again to check Ollie's condition, but instead of confirming Ollie's breathing, Flint gently laid him down next to a small rock piling.

"I don't want to stop, but we need to build a fire and rest anyways. I'm not sure he will make it through the night without the warmth of a fire." He began gathering up small twigs and bits of dried brush.

As he urged his kindling to catch fire, I knelt over Ollie. He looked even worse than before. His lips were blue and his face was swollen on the right side where he must have hit a rock during his fall. Having only my jacket as a remedy, I took it off and tied it to Flint's coat, creating a jacket cocoon for Ollie.

The combined heat of the fire and jackets brought some color back to his skin, but he was still unresponsive. His lips quivered gently, but no comprehensible words came out. I tried talking to him to lift his spirits, but I wasn't sure if he could even hear me. Ollie was going to need more than warmth to recover from his injuries.

With nothing left to do but wait until morning, I huddled up in front of the fire with Ollie. Anxious and restless, I found myself popping my head up with every sound in the night, which caused me to strain my neck. Too often, I realized that the sound I heard was coming from my own restless movement.

My stomach growled. I had no desire for food while we walked, but my hunger became overwhelmingly clear as the night dragged on. I reached for my backpack to see what snacks I had. After a quick look around us, I realized that it must have fallen off when we were ambushed.

Not only was I hungry, tired, and sore; I was also physically and emotionally depleted. Thinking of my own exhaustion left me full of guilt. How could I feel sorry for myself as I sat next to Ollie, who may never wake up?

I hugged my knees and let my head fall. I did not realize Flint had gotten up until I felt something pressing into my hand. I looked up to see that I was holding a chunk of bread. Flint stood on the other side of the fire eating the other half.

"You need calories if you want to finish the hike tomorrow."

I nodded my head once in gratitude as I devoured my small piece of bread. My hunger once again became manageable, which left me feeling somewhat rejuvenated and I found myself drifting to sleep.

I jolted awake when I felt a consistent gentle breeze go by. It felt as if a fan was going side to side across my face. One moment I felt the breeze and the next it was gone. Flint was throwing his daggers, one by one, into the darkness. When he ran out of daggers, he walked straight into the darkness. Moments later, he re-appeared with his daggers and a handful of small lizards. He began cooking them over the fire.

"It's not much, but it will help." He sounded dejected.

While he tended to our main course, which roasted slowly over the open flames, he handed me his knives.

I began throwing them, one after the other, like he had been doing. Concentrating and throwing. Concentrating and throwing. I tried to enlarge my pupils the way Ollie showed me, but nothing happened. I was left with a massive headache on top of my exhaustion. I took a break from the knives so I could eat my desert lizard. Flint said it would taste like chicken, but I was certain it tasted like lizard. I had no complaints. In my exhausted state, food was food.

After picking through the lizard, Flint rolled to his side and his breathing evened out immediately. Alone with my thoughts, I went back to practicing with his knives. I threw them into the darkness of the night. I hit nothing, but I did get better at finding discarded knives in the dark. I could hear the exact location of each knife as it hit the dirt. At least I was getting better at something.

Hours passed. When my arm got too tired to throw, I took a break to sit with Ollie until the night burned away. I assumed the sun was starting to rise, but when I looked towards the horizon there was nothing to indicate that dawn was coming. The stars and the moon were still out. They were barely visible through the clouds, but their light shone through. I could see everything around me as if it was all behind a thin curtain.

I knew the next day would be exhausting and I wanted to get some sleep, but I couldn't stop thinking about Ollie. I was worried about my friend. He had become like a little brother to me since I arrived. Having spent so many years looking out for myself, I struggled with the feeling of helplessness and my inability to do anything to fix this for him. My anxious mind woke me up every fifteen minutes to check on him. No changes.

I continued to stoke the fire throughout the night to ensure Ollie was warm. The size of the flames was the only thing I had control over. Flint would occasionally peek at the two of us from across the fire. Since there was nothing we could do for Ollie until morning, I think Flint was mostly checking to make sure I didn't do something rash out of desperation.

CHAPTER 10
THE INFIRMARY

The temperature rose to triple digits shortly after sunrise, which would have forced us to get an early start even if we weren't already in a rush to bring Ollie back to The Sanctuary. We kept looking down at Ollie as Flint dragged his stretcher behind us, but his eyes remained swollen shut.

The only noise coming from his mouth was raspy breath from the dry desert air. I had taken my jacket off of him as soon as it became too warm for it, and held it up in an attempt to protect him from the blistering sun.

We arrived at The Sanctuary before noon and immediately started shouting for help. Others came to help us carry Ollie's stretcher to the infirmary, which allowed us to move much faster.

Somebody must have notified the doctors that we were coming, because a woman was waiting for us outside the infirmary along with the man who had helped me with my wrist and another man. She ordered the two men to bring Ollie inside and gently lay him on a bed. I followed them inside, but only made it a few steps before the woman told me sternly that guests waited outside.

In the hallway, I slid down the wall in a heap of desperation and exhaustion. Flint sat next to me, but the others had gone back to their duties as soon as the infirmary doors were closed. It seemed odd that they wouldn't stay to make sure Ollie was okay, but I guess standing in this hallway wouldn't help him heal any faster.

After a few minutes, somebody came down the hallway with two cups of water and some bread. They put it down in front of us and left without a word. I wasn't hungry, but I couldn't resist the water after spending all morning in the hot sun.

As we waited anxiously outside the room, Flint assured me that Ollie was in good hands. I was not convinced. One of the men had barely helped me with my wrist, and the woman didn't look like any doctor I had ever seen. Her hair was buzzed on one side and long on the other, and she wore a sleeveless shirt that showcased all of the tattoos covering her left side.

Leaning his head against the wall, Flint told me that Sierra hadn't come to The Sanctuary until a couple years ago.

"After Stratus attempted to destroy The Heightened over a decade ago, Sierra and her husband moved to Prague. They erased any connection to the rest of us. They built a new life, using their medical training to open a small walk-in clinic.

"They had been there for six years when Stratus found them. They were walking home one night, taking the same path they took every time. As they turned the corner to their home, they were ambushed.

"They fought the men as long as they could, but they were losing. When her husband screamed for her to run, she did. She thought he would be right behind her, but he had stayed behind to prevent them from following her. When she looked back, he was gone, along with Stratus's men."

He described how Sierra had spent two years hacking government databases, dissecting the dark web, and calling in every favor owed to her, but couldn't find any trace of Stratus or her husband.

"She made her way here, and has been our medic ever since," he finished.

We sat in silence for a few minutes until the door opened. We jumped up to find the man who had given me the wrist brace. He greeted Flint with a nod, then held the door open. With nobody stopping me, I practically ran into the infirmary.

Ollie didn't look much better than he did before. A bit cleaner, maybe, but that only served to highlight his bruises. Sierra told us that she was able to stabilize Ollie's vitals, but she could not tell us if, or when, he would wake up.

I felt like the floor had fallen out from underneath me. I tried to hold in my emotions, feeling self-conscious about my grief in a room full of strangers.

When I saw Flint standing at the foot of the bed with misty eyes, it was like my chest cracked in half. His pain made mine impossible to ignore. I didn't want to lose my friend.

This place was supposed to be *safe*.

Sierra moved so she stood next to Flint, and gently took his hand. He closed his eyes and hung his head as he took a deep breath and softly squeezed her hand in return. I knew he felt responsible for everything that had happened in the up-top, since he was the most experienced one in our group, but anybody who was there would agree that he did everything he could.

When he raised his head, his face was stoic once more. He let go of Sierra's hand and gestured from me to her.

"I should introduce you. Kai, this is my sister. Sierra, this is the kid I told you about." Said Flint.

Shocked out of my grief, I gaped for a moment as my brain tried to process that the two of them were related. Flint had a sister who, by the way, looked nothing like him.

"Thank you for helping Ollie. Flint said you're the best there is, and I'm really happy you're here, because Ollie deserves the best, and I really need him to wake up and be okay, and I didn't even know Flint had a sister, but here you are, so thank you and *please* fix him." I said, my emotions making me babble.

Sierra smiled warmly at me. "It's nice to meet you too Kai, and I will do everything I can to help Ollie. As for Flint forgetting to mention me, well he has always been like that, even when we were kids." Sierra turned to her brother and scrunched up her nose.

"He told me you were looking for something. Remind me to show you when things are less precarious," she said gently.

I suddenly became aware of several people outside the door. My initial reaction was panic that Stratus's men had found us again, but Flint and Sierra seemed more exasperated than worried.

Listening more closely, I began to make out individual voices. Word had spread rapidly about Ollie's condition and Jax's unknown whereabouts. Everybody wanted to know what had happened, and whether the safety of The Sanctuary had been compromised.

My ears picked up the staccato of one heart, which beat harder and faster than the rest. She burst into the room like the door had been made of paper instead of bound wood.

Hurricane Sam stopped immediately and her hands flew to her mouth as she caught sight of Ollie. Sam was shaking as she reached out to take Ollie's hand in hers, whispering, "please please please" as if she could wake him up by will alone.

Sierra suggested that Flint and I wash the dirt off of us, then she signaled to the two men who had helped bring Ollie in. The four of us slipped quietly into the hallway so Sam and Sierra could have a moment of privacy.

Estes approached as soon as the large wood doors closed behind us. He must have convinced everybody else to leave, because the hallway was suspiciously empty of the voices I had heard minutes before. Jax's kidnapping had caused panic to spread like wildfire. What was believed to be an impenetrable fortress was suddenly vulnerable, and the people were terrified.

"We have already sent a group to destroy the tracks you created on the way back here." Estes put his hand on Flint's shoulder as Flint let out a sigh of relief. "There will be an emergency Elder Forum tomorrow to address the hysteria."

Estes informed Flint and me that our attendance would be mandatory, since we were the only people who could explain what had happened. The Elders promised that they would secure everybody's safety. After seeing the way Stratus's men overtook us, I didn't believe safety was a promise they would be able to keep.

Flint immediately agreed to go to the meeting. He wanted to take down Stratus more than anyone. I was not excited at the prospect of being interrogated. All I wanted was a large cup of water and a nap, but I would do anything to help Ollie. Much as I didn't like him, we also needed to find Jax.

CHAPTER 11
ONE STEP CLOSER

The next day, I sat on the floor of Estes's room and waited for the sun to rise. The moment a tiny golden speck of light peeked through the cracks, I jumped up and ran to the infirmary.

I slipped through the heavy doors and found Sam sitting half in her chair and half on Ollie's bed. Realizing that she spent the night there, and feeling like I was intruding, I slipped back out and made my way to the dining hall. It was early enough that most people were still in their rooms, which allowed me to avoid interaction as I stacked food onto a tray and brought it back down the hallway.

When I opened the infirmary doors with Sam's food cradled in one hand, I found Sierra standing over Ollie. She smiled at Sam. That was promising. I put the tray next to Sam, then took the only other available chair in the room which was on the other side of Ollie. Sierra told Sam that Ollie's heart rate was stable and that there was no swelling in his brain. She checked a few more charts before patting Sam on the shoulder and turning to me.

"I'll be back every hour to check on him," she said gently before leaving us alone.

Sam and I were with Ollie all day. Flint, Estes, and a few others stopped by to bring food and check on him. As promised, Sierra came back every hour to check Ollie's vitals. Each time she entered, I watched anxiously until she turned to give Sam and me a smile. That smile was our confirmation that Ollie was stable. He didn't seem to be getting better, but at least he wasn't getting worse.

As the day wore on, some of the color returned to his cheeks. It was a promising sign, but it also gave more vibrance to the dark bruises and swelling across his face. Ollie looked like he was asleep, his bruise-stained body tucked under the sheets with only his arms and face peeking out. I wanted to look at the bed and see his brown eyes alive with excitement, but instead I was greeted with the sight of several tubes sticking out of his bruised arms.

I wondered how they found us. Had Flint and I been careless when we came, or was Stratus following a different trail? I must have fallen asleep while pondering this, because I woke up to the sound of feet shuffling across the floor. Flint. I looked up to find Sam asleep with her face next to Ollie's, holding his hand like it was the only thing tethering her to this world. I turned to Flint and saw him place our dinner next to the untouched meals from breakfast and lunch. He let me know that Sierra had just left and that the meeting would start in about an hour.

As he was walking out the door, several of Ollie's friends came into the room. Sam was instantly awake, and we both moved back a bit to make space for them. They sat on the bed near Ollie's feet and told him all of the rumors they had heard; that he ran away, that he fought Stratus himself, and most bittersweet, that he had woken up.

I heard a small ping as they jostled each other for the chance to regale him with stories, and was worried that they had disturbed one of the many tubes providing Ollie with medicine and fluids. Judging by the way Sam jumped up and meticulously checked his arms, I assumed she had the same thoughts. Once she was satisfied that everything was in order, she sat back down.

I walked over to the food tray and grabbed a roll, which I offered to Sam as I sat next to her. She stared at it like she didn't know what it was, but after a few minutes she gently took it from me. Picking tiny pieces off and rolling them into balls before chewing on them, she told me that Ollie might be able to hear his friends.

"Last night after you left, I asked Sierra what I could do to help. She told me to talk to him. I guess some people in a coma," she choked out the last word, "can remember what you said. You know, after they wake up. They remember."

I didn't know how to respond to that. It sounded like something fake that you said to cheer somebody up, but Sierra didn't seem like the type of person to lie about Ollie's condition just to make Sam feel better.

"I'm happy they came. I am sure he loves all of this attention." She rolled another small piece of bread into a ball and gave me a sad smile. "Thank you for coming. I am sure it means a lot to him that you've spent all day here."

I noticed she was talking about Ollie like he really could hear us, and that he would wake up at any moment. She probably wasn't able to consider the alternative, whereas it's almost all I thought about.

I reached out and held her hand in silence. Two people holding out hope for the same thing.

Sierra came back and shooed Ollie's friends out, but that also meant it was time for me to leave for the meeting. As I stood up, I saw something shiny on the floor by Ollie's bed.

Sam and Sierra were so wrapped up in their discussion of Ollie's health that they didn't notice me bend down to pick it up. It looked like a military dog tag. My stomach sank. The only soldiers I had encountered recently were the ones who did this to Ollie. I stood and shoved the dog tag into my pocket, realizing that Ollie's friends must have knocked it loose from his pocket when they were on his bed.

I needed to talk to Flint. Hoping the look on my face came off as nervousness about the emergency meeting, I excused myself and headed towards the dining hall. Surely somebody there would point me in the right direction.

CHAPTER 12
THE FUTURE OF THE SANCTUARY

I found myself standing outside a small room. The meeting should have been held in a room that could accommodate the entire Sanctuary, since it appeared that everybody was in attendance except the three I left at the infirmary. Instead, they held it in the Elder Room. Not a very original name, but the people of The Sanctuary were nothing if not practical.

As soon as I entered, I was pushed to the front of the room. I stumbled into the only available space, which was next to Flint on a podium. In hindsight, the space was probably empty because it was reserved for me.

I turned towards the elders, seated at a place of honor on a second podium. I expected them to take turns asking us questions. Instead, we were barraged with questions from the audience. The questions were shouted at us so quickly and by so many people, it was hard to pick just one question to answer.

"Where is Jax?" Someone shouted from the crowd.

"I don't know," I responded honestly while Flint stood stoically next to me.

"Does he know we are here?" Another member asked, their voice shrill with panic.

"When will Ollie wake up?"

"Where did they go?"

"Will they be back?"

"Should we leave?"

"I don't know." My voice was barely audible above the noise of the crowd.

"What do you know?" One of the elders yelled, which silenced the crowd as they waited patiently for my answer.

Flint took a step forward, partially shielding me from the Elders as he told them everything he could remember about the attack. Three men. Two motorcycles. Military clothing. Jax was injected with a sedative. They were waiting for us, which means they knew we would be there, and yes, they might know about The Sanctuary.

At that last admission, the crowd became even louder than before. The future of The Sanctuary was at stake and everyone wanted to keep themselves and their family safe from another massacre like the one that happened a decade ago.

The Elders were divided between two groups. One claimed the threat was false and encouraged everybody to carry on as usual. The other group suggested that they find another place to live immediately.

The only Elder who agreed with Flint was Estes. The two of them argued that we should all be searching for Jax and bringing the fight to Stratus.

Flint's voice rose above the shouted arguments.

"Heightened do not hide. We do not cower in fear. The Sanctuary was never meant to be permanent. Do not raise another generation underground. No more running. We must bring the fight to *them* this time. We can end this once and for all, if we work together."

Barton was not amused. Slamming his cane on the table, he blamed Flint for Jax's abduction and Stratus's knowledge of The Sanctuary.

"You! You do not get to judge us for our unwillingness to risk more lives. It was you who was reckless. You, who brought them here, and now the rest of us are paying the price."

There was a moment of stunned silence, then the crowd erupted. Each person was screaming at each other. The fear and worry that had been directed at us from the beginning had turned into anger and disgust with each other. As the tension grew and the noise became nearly unbearable, Flint gently pulled me off the podium and guided me towards the back of the room where Sierra was standing near the doorway.

He turned his back on us and headed back towards the podium, leaving me with Sierra as he squeezed through the angry mob.

All at once, the tension evaporated. It was like the room let out a sigh, as everybody's hands lowered, faces relaxed, and voices quieted. In the silence, the council unanimously decided to end the meeting early and discuss the matter at a later time. The entire group all turned towards Sierra and me as they made their way to the back of the room. One by one, they left the Elder Room. Still standing with his back to us, Flint waited until the entire room was empty before turning to face us. He looked like he was about to explode, and I wondered briefly if he had absorbed the fury of the entire room.

Storming up to Sierra, he grabbed her arm and practically dragged her into the nearest sound-holder.

"What were you thinking," he whisper-shouted in her face, the sound barely audible to me even though I stood right outside the soundproof closet.

Standing her ground, Sierra spoke gently and clearly. "Sometimes people just need a break, Flint. Emotion clouds judgment."

"You were careless," he spat.

Sierra looked down at her hands and took a deep breath, then she looked him dead in the eye and spoke with conviction.

"No. I was careful. We are done talking about this here. If you would like to have this conversation after you have had the chance to calm down, you know where to find me."

Flint threw his hands in the air and stalked out of the room.

I needed to tell Flint about the dog tag, but his explosion hinted to me that this was a bad time. Sierra watched him leave, then turned to me.

"I'm headed back to check on Ollie, if you'd like to join me."

She didn't say anything as she guided me in the direction of the infirmary. Her appearance and gentle personality were so different from Flint that it was hard to believe they were related. In the quiet hallway, with her pursed lips and dipped brow, their resemblance was glaringly obvious. It was the same expression I saw on his face throughout our entire journey to The Sanctuary.

I was so busy replaying their argument in my head that I was not paying attention to our surroundings. I snapped back to reality when I felt a cold breeze coming through a small star-shaped crack. We were in an unfamiliar tunnel. Fighting the panic rising in my stomach, I turned to Sierra.

"It's okay," she assured me, though the way she kept looking over my shoulder said otherwise. "Nobody can hear us down here, but we have to be quick."

"Quick about what?" I asked, worried that I had done something wrong.

"Hush now and listen. Did Flint tell you that some Heightened are more powerful than others? No, of course he wouldn't. Well, some of us have supernatural abilities. It is rare, but when it does happen, these people are seen as extremely dangerous, even by other Heightened." She froze and cocked her head, squinting down the hallway. Seemingly satisfied that we were alone, she continued.

"I can change your mood. I won't unless I need to, but I can alter the hormone levels in your body and give you the feelings I want you to have."

I sucked in a breath, but she continued before my mouth could form the questions my brain wanted answers to.

"After my husband was captured, I looked into every lead I had. As each one turned out to be a dead end, I sank deeper into depression. Then there were construction workers making noise outside my bedroom window, just doing their jobs, but my anger was uncontrollable. I started screaming at them. One thing led to another, we caused a scene, then they just *stopped*. They apologized and decided to take their lunch break. Then it happened again at the laundromat, and again at the market. I was changing the mood of people around me, and therefore changing their behavior."

There had been so many surprises in my life over the past month that I no longer felt shocked about anything. The only surprise was that my fellow Heightened would be afraid of her instead of seeing her as a leader. Realizing that other people in my new life might also have these special abilities, my heart soared. Maybe we had an even better chance at beating Stratus than I thought.

"Is Flint like you?" I asked enthusiastically.

"No. None of the people down here are, or they hide it like I do. We think some of the women killed during the Salem witch trials might have been like me, but we don't like to talk about that. Heightened have been hunted over and over throughout history for being what we are. There is a real fear that one of us with abilities greater than a typical Heightened would only cause us to be hunted down more aggressively. I would be cast out, in order to protect the others." She looked at me intently.

"Flint is the only person who I have told. I suspect that Estes has figured it out, but he is too much of a gentleman to ask me outright. If the rest knew, they would banish me without a second thought."

"Why are you telling me?" I asked, wondering what I had done to earn the level of secrecy only held by her brother.

"Flint trusts you, so I trust you." Sierra responded matter of factly, then glanced over my shoulder again and lowered her voice. "I also know that Flint will go after Stratus. He will tell me to stay behind where it is safe. When that day comes, you need to convince him to bring me. My abilities would be a huge advantage if I can get close enough."

She looked into my eyes. Seeming satisfied with what she saw, she took my arm and walked to the infirmary like nothing had happened.

I wondered if I should tell Sierra about the dog tag. She trusted me with a secret that could ruin her life, so she had earned the right to know what I had found in her infirmary. Somehow, I couldn't bring myself to tell her. I assured myself that I would tell her as soon as I got a chance to look at it. Maybe it was nothing at all, though my gut said it was something. A very important something.

After confirming that Ollie was stable and making sure Sam didn't need anything, I headed back to Estes's room. I had been hoping to find Flint, but the room was empty. I lit a fire and sat with my back to the small doorway. Using my body as a wall to hide the treasure from anybody that might come in, I pulled the dog tag out of my pocket.

One side of the tag read James R. Stevens with the numbers 618-531-303 while the other side said EVOLVE in large letters, taking up nearly the entire space. Flipping it back and forth, I didn't see any other words or markings.

Holding the dog tag in my palm, I rubbed the bottom of my thumb across it as I wondered how many people in the world had the name James R. Stevens, and whether it would even be possible to track them all down. It might not even be a real name, and if it was, I was sure Stratus had the desire and ability to hide the identities of his operatives.

I jerked my hand back when my thumb ran across a sharp corner and drew blood. Realizing I had another clue, I looked closer, but all I saw was a slightly worn corner. I deflated as my brief moment of hope slipped away. There were no secret codes or markings. It was probably scratched when Ollie pulled it off of the man, or when they fell from the motorcycle.

One name. One number. One word.

I hoped that Flint would come back soon, and that he would be able to decipher the dog tag's secrets.

CHAPTER 13
THE TRUTH

I woke up on the floor next to a cold fire. I must have fallen asleep waiting for Flint. His hammock had been disturbed, which meant he had come and gone without waking me. I guess superpowers don't work when you're out cold, which reminded me of Ollie.

I grabbed a tray of food from the dining hall, shoving a roll in my mouth and jogging to the infirmary. I hoped Sam would eat something more than tiny bread balls.

Flint caught up to me just as I arrived at the large wooden doors. I must have been so deep in my thoughts that I didn't hear him coming, because his sudden presence startled me.

"Kai, I need a minute with you." Flint placed his hand over mine on the door to prevent me from opening it.

"Of course, I wanted to talk to you anyways," I responded, taking a step away from the door. Flint walked down the hall a bit, and I guessed that he expected me to follow him.

"I don't think it will be safe to stay here much longer." Flint whispered so quietly that I had to rely on lip reading and facial expressions to fully understand what he was saying.

"What? Why?" I whispered back, though it was much louder than his whisper.

"Because," Flint looked at the floor like it was his fault. "I know why they captured Jax."

I found myself moving closer to Flint until Sam's tray was touching his stomach. I stared at his mouth, as if begging it to continue telling me what he knew.

"A few months before you met me, I was tracking some of Stratus's men. My goal was to gain information about their headquarters. Instead, I discovered something much worse."

I nodded slowly, encouraging him to finish this story.

"I thought they were using an abandoned apartment complex as their base in Chicago. After several weeks of surveillance, I decided to go in for a closer look during one of their guard shifts. When I got to the basement, I realized it was not a hideout. Hospital beds were evenly spaced along the walls, separated only by thin blue curtains. Each bed held a man. They were all strapped to the bed, frail, and unconscious. They looked like they had been tortured for days. They were barely breathing, the air moved through their lungs so quietly that only a dog, or a Heightened, could hear it. I knew I only had a moment before the guards caught me, so I grabbed some paperwork from the table closest to me and I left."

"You just left them to die?" I interrupted, my voice rising to a shrill whisper that I was sure other Heightened would be able to hear if they were awake.

"There was nothing I could do by myself. They were too weak to leave on their own, and there were too many of them for me to move without being captured myself. I sent copies of the paperwork to Estes, then I went back. At least if I went missing, he would be able to follow the trail." Flint ran his hands through his hair, something I had never seen him do.

"The building was empty. Four hours, and there was no trace of them." Flint continued in a tone of remorse, as if he was re-living the helplessness of that day.

"What were they doing?" I knew the answer must be important, but I was still afraid of what he would say.

"Experiments. Tests. Trying to make an army by increasing their regular human abilities to make them into…" Flint trailed off as he pointed between the two of us.

"An army of Heightened." I suddenly found it hard to breathe. If Stratus had a small team of Heightened, we would never be able to rescue Jax without risking more of us being captured or killed. If he had an entire army? There weren't enough of us to put up any kind of resistance.

We were dead. Ollie. Sam. Sierra. Estes. All of us.

"I don't think any of those men survived. The paperwork I found said it was his 27th experiment, and the paperwork doesn't indicate that any of the previous 26 survived. His team needed more information on our cellular structure. If I'm right, it's the reason they came here. In order to create a successful formula for Heightened, they would have needed-" he looked me in the eyes, probably hoping he wouldn't have to finish the sentence.

"They knew. They knew where to find us. The Sanctuary. They knew and they just waited." It felt like my brain had stopped working. I was excited to have superhero powers. I was excited to be in The Sanctuary. I was excited to meet other Heightened. I was excited to train, even when I was injured. It had been a lot to take in, but I was eager for more.

Now, I wish I didn't know any of it.

I wanted to go back to Hope Street, where the risks were consistent. Where nobody wanted to perform experiments on my friends. Where nobody wanted to kill me. Where nobody wanted to take over the world with a manufactured superhero army.

Sam's tray slipped for a moment, spilling half of her food onto the ground before I righted it.

I could feel my breath becoming shallow, my lungs struggling for air as the light in the hall seemed to dim with each loud heartbeat coming from my chest. I wanted to ask if the Elders knew about the experiments, but I could only gasp out a few words at a time.

"Tell the Elders." Labored inhale.

"I was going to tell them last night, but things got out of control at the meeting. I will tell them today," said Flint.

"Who knows?" Labored inhale.

"Are you okay, Kai? I think you need to calm down."

"Who knows?" I said more loudly before taking another labored inhale.

"Estes and Sierra. The rest of The Sanctuary won't respond well. We will get Jax back." Flint said quickly, then took the tray from me and guided me to the infirmary.

He led me to the chair next to Ollie, which only made me feel worse as I looked at my unconscious friend who had barely escaped becoming a human experiment.

Sierra came around the corner the moment I sat down. She squatted in front of me and took my hands in hers, raising my hands a few inches as she took deep breaths, then lowering my hands again as she let out the air. It was like I had forgotten what breathing was supposed to look like and she needed to show me.

I don't know how long we stayed like that, but eventually my breathing slowed down enough that I didn't feel like I was drowning in my own skin. As I began to calm down, I realized that I didn't see Sam or Flint in the room. I turned to peer around Sierra, then behind me, but they were gone.

She must have known who I was looking for, because she answered the question before I even spoke it.

"Sam was starting to smell." She gave me a crooked smile, probably hoping to lighten the mood. "I sent her to wash off and get her own breakfast this morning. Don't worry, she left before you and Estes started arguing in the hallway."

I nodded and continued breathing slowly, following our hands.

"Sounds like you had quite the morning. Do you want to talk about it?"

I shook my head.

"Well, Flint went looking for Sam so he could keep her away from here for a bit. Give you some privacy. I think he felt bad for putting all that information in your little head first thing in the morning, as he should! Imagine telling a child that a whole army is out to kill everybody they love. I swear, that man has no sense sometimes."

At this, I did smile. Only Sierra could make Flint sound oblivious.

"So you heard us, then?" I felt like I should be embarrassed by my outburst in the hallway, but I also felt like I was handling this information remarkably well.

"Oh honey, I think even Ollie heard you." The light in her eyes said she was teasing me, but I couldn't resist looking at Ollie.

Something was different about him. It took me a moment to notice, but most of the tubes had been removed from his arm. Afraid to hope for good news, I voiced the same question I had been asking since we got back.

"Is he awake?" I stood up on shaky legs and took a step towards him.

"He woke up a few times last night. Got really worked up about some necklace, so I gave him a sedative. He's not quite healed yet, and I can't have him injuring himself further on my watch. Anyways, it should wear off soon if you want to stick around."

She turned to walk away before pausing and turning back to me.

"I don't want you to feel violated. Just now, with the breathing, I didn't *use* anything. It was just a regular breathing exercise. Nothing else."

I smiled and thanked her, understanding what she was hinting at.

CHAPTER 14
WAKING UP

It felt like a weight had been pressing on my chest ever since the attack, growing heavier and heavier each day. Flint's information about Stratus had been the final piece of pressure to completely crush me, but Sierra's words allowed me to breathe deeply again for the first time in days.

Flint walked in with Sam.

Sierra smiled at Sam, but turned and raised her eyebrows admonishingly at Flint before checking Ollie's vitals.

"Kai, I apologize for what I did this morning," he said to me as he eyed Sam. Satisfied that she was clueless about the incident, he announced that he would be in a meeting with Barton if there was any change to Ollie's status.

I watched Sierra move methodically around Ollie, only then noticing the bags under her eyes. She must have been up all night to keep him stable as he woke up. She removed the final tube from his arm, making him look like he really was just sleeping.

Pleased with his health, she told us that she would be sleeping in her chamber next door if we needed her.

"It shouldn't be long now," she said as she walked to the door. "You know where to find me if something happens." We nodded and she was gone.

Alone with Sam, I pulled my chair around so we were sitting on the same side of Ollie's bed. Even though she had eaten and washed, she still looked exhausted. The only difference was that she didn't look quite so hopeless now. She almost looked content as she waited for the sedatives to wear off. Almost.

We sat in comfortable silence, each stuck in our own heads. I had a lot of information to process now that I could breathe again.

Each time Ollie stirred, we threw ourselves at the bed to fret over him, but he never fully woke up.

I offered to get lunch from the dining hall, but Sam claimed that she was still full from breakfast. Apparently Flint had convinced her to eat more than her stomach was ready for, and it was still recuperating from the feeling of fullness after so many days surviving on bread balls.

I woke up annoyed at whomever was flicking me on the arm. Jerking away from the offender, I opened my eyes to find Ollie staring at me.

I had never been more relieved.

In pure Ollie fashion, he pelted me with questions before I could even ask how he was feeling. Despite his still-swollen face and raspy voice, he spoke so fast that it was like one single sentence.

"Where's Flint? What happened? Where's Jax? What time is it? I'm starving. Is there anything to eat? Why are we in this room? She looks gross. Who put bandages on my arm?"

Sam woke up near the end of his tirade, just in time to hear him comment on her appearance. I laughed as I watched her face melt from elation to irritation, and back to elation before she started laughing too. Sam launched herself at the bed, throwing her arms around Ollie as tears of relief slid down her face.

I processed his questions. Ollie had missed some of the most eventful days in The Sanctuary.

"Sam, you're going to squeeze me to death," he said through giggles, though Sam showed no signs of releasing him. It was good to hear his laugh again.

Bending sideways so he could see me through Sam's hug, I asked Ollie about the last thing he remembers before he woke up.

He thought for a minute. "We went to the up-top. Jax and Flint came too!" He stopped as the memories seemed to flood back into him.

Looking terrified, he whispered "Oh. The man." After an unusually long period of silence for Ollie, he continued. "He wanted to take me away, and I tried to fight, but he was too strong and he had a *real* motorcycle."

Sam looked up at me with worry in her eyes. Telling him the truth would crush him, but it was better that he found out from us than to wander The Sanctuary catching bits and pieces of gossip over the next few days.

"Who was it?" Ollie asked.

Sam buried her face in Ollie's neck, so I answered.

I tried to answer his question with the truth that I knew yesterday, without mistakenly revealing the truth that Flint had dumped on me that morning.

"We think it was one of Stratus's men. You were so brave, and you fought so well. You totally scared that guy off, but you fell really hard and hit your head. Flint and I carried you back here so Sierra could help you." I glanced back at Sam and continued, "You have been unconscious for a few days."

"Wow! I fought off one of Stratus's men. I can't wait to tell my friends! I bet Flint and Jax were really impressed." Ollie said, clearly thrilled with the idea that he was able to defeat one of Stratus's men.

Seeing the look on my face, Ollie deflated before nervously asking, "What else happened?"

"Well, your friends came to visit you. They all think you're really brave."

"What else?" Ollie must have known I was stalling.

"Flint just left, but he should be back soon. He will be so excited to see you awake." I told him.

"What about Jax?" Ollie's voice was becoming hysterical and I knew I had to say the words that I was dreading.

I suppose I should have expected that he would want to know what happened while he was unconscious. I had been so focused on whether he would wake up that I didn't think about what I would say to him when he *did* wake up. I looked to Sam for guidance, but she seemed to deflate as she sat back in her chair and held his hand comfortingly.

As I opened my mouth, I heard Sam's quiet voice as she answered Ollie.

"He's gone, but we're safe now, and we'll find him."

I didn't think we were safe in The Sanctuary, and I didn't know which "we" were going to find him, but I was grateful that she had been the one to tell him.

"What do you mean he's *gone*," he shrieked.

Realizing I had to give him more information before the rest of The Sanctuary heard him and came running, I started talking.

"There were other men. They took Jax, the way they tried to take you." Not wanting to disparage his hero, I explained, "one of them had a needle, so I think they gave him something to make him sleepy. We had a meeting with the Elders, but it got a bit out of hand with everybody yelling at each other." I moved again, so my face was directly in front of his. Staring into his tear lined eyes, I made a promise that I hoped I would be able to keep.

"Hey buddy, we *will* get him back. Flint is coming up with a plan with the Elders right now." I tried to sound confident and hopeful, though I felt anything but.

The three of us sat in silence for a few minutes before I remembered that we were supposed to wake Sierra. Realizing I could never ask Sam to leave him, I stood to leave.

Ollie had an immediate reaction when he realized I was going to leave the infirmary. This usually fearless boy was terrified that I wouldn't come back. I tried to reassure him that I was only going to wake Sierra, but it didn't seem to comfort him at all.

Sam saved me by distracting him with stories about all of his friends who had come to visit, which allowed me to slip out the door. He saw me go, but didn't argue.

Walking down the hall, I wondered how long his fear would last. The whole Sanctuary had vibrated with fear and worry ever since we had returned, and they weren't even involved in the incident.

I turned the corner and bumped right into Sierra. Seeing me walking around, she asked if Ollie was awake.

"He woke up a few minutes ago. He's with Sam, but we had to tell him what happened. I don't know if you can help him, but…" I let the words die on my tongue as she closed her eyes and hung her head.

I didn't know how much I needed the warm hug that she wrapped around me, but my body seemed to melt into it. "The poor kid's been through so much. I'll do what I can, but some things just need time." She continued holding me for a few more seconds, then stepped back to look at me with her hands on my shoulders.

"You don't need to carry this weight by yourself. Ollie belongs to The Sanctuary, and everybody here will do what they can to help." She gave me a small smile and a final squeeze of my shoulders, then she turned and walked to the infirmary.

I took a step to follow her, but remembered my promise to Ollie. I really hoped that Flint's meeting was successful and that he had a plan to rescue Jax.

Turning on my heel, I headed to the Elder Room. The room felt much bigger when it wasn't full of people screaming at each other.

I found Flint in Estes's room.

"What did Barton say?" I whispered, though I don't know why I bothered when everybody could probably hear me anyways. Habit, I guess.

Flint frowned down at me.

"It went just how I expected. He won't put together a rescue party to find Jax. When I told him that Estes and I would go, he didn't try to talk us out of it. His only demand was that we didn't tell the rest of The Sanctuary of our plan. It looks like it will be up to the two of us." Flint continued.

"What about Sierra?" I asked, realizing she had been right to assume he would leave without her.

"Absolutely not. It's too dangerous." Flint responded immediately, as if the answer was obvious.

"You really think you can stop her? At least this way you know where she is, instead of having her follow you across the globe." I said.

"Who will run the infirmary? Somebody needs to keep an eye on Ollie." Using Ollie as an excuse to keep her here would have worked, but he didn't know that Ollie was already awake.

"Actually, Sierra said Ollie is stable enough to leave the infirmary tomorrow."

Flint looked at the ceiling and shook his head. He didn't like it, but he had no valid reason to keep Sierra behind. Besides, her special gift would be really helpful if he was ambushed again. If we were ambushed.

"There is something else that I need to talk to you about, but first you need to know that I'm coming."

"That's even more ridiculous!" He actually shouted. I guessed that we were done whispering, so I responded in a normal speaking voice.

Did I miss Jax? No, but he was part of this group - *my* group - and if I could help bring back Ollie's hero, I would do it. For him.

"I have nothing here. You are the closest thing I have to family, and Jax getting captured was just as much my fault as it was yours. Besides, I might be able to get intel that you can't. Nobody suspects teenagers of being spies." I paused for a moment. "If you say no, I'll follow you anyways just like Sierra would."

"No." He almost growled the word.

"Fine," I began, then decided to silently mouth the rest of my threat to him. "I won't tell you about the dog tag I found." I raised my eyebrows in defiance as I waited for his response.

He glared at me, weighing his odds. It didn't take long for him to hold his hand out, palm up.

I smiled in triumph and pulled the small piece of metal from my pocket. I placed it in his hand, and he immediately turned his back to the hallway to protect it from intrusive eyes like I had done the night before.

"When Ollie's friends were in the infirmary yesterday, they were messing around and-" I was cut off as he grabbed me by the hand, making me wince.

"Sorry, I forgot you hurt that one." His apology was more of a desperate plea for me to keep moving than a remorseful statement, as he grabbed my other hand and practically sprinted to the sound-holder.

"Anyways, Ollie's friends made this fall off of his bed. He must have grabbed it from *Mr. Stevens*," I paused for a moment to emphasize that we knew the man's name, "when he was trying to take Ollie."

"Do you know what this means?" Flint asked rhetorically. He never looked up from the tag. I wondered if this was the same look I had on my face when I found it in Ollie's hand.

"If we can find this," he looked down at the name, "*James* person's military files, we may be able to find Jax. This could give us the upper hand for the first time in years."

Flint seemed to come back to himself, and turned to me "We leave first thing in the morning."

Before I could respond, he was gone.

CHAPTER 15
FAREWELL

I didn't have anything to pack, so I spent the rest of the day with Ollie.

He had a constant flow of visitors once word got out that he was awake. While he was excited to see everybody, it took a toll. Sam had to kick people out of the infirmary several times through the afternoon so Ollie could rest.

After everything he had been through, it wouldn't have been right to leave without saying goodbye. I knew this, yet I was dreading that conversation. I didn't know what words to use, or how to convince him that he should stay behind, because I knew he would want to come with us just like I had wanted to come.

It was late and I still hadn't mustered the courage to tell him.

He was currently playing a game on his bed. Ollie and Sam took turns bouncing a small rubber ball off of the flat wooden board that was sitting across Ollie's legs.

Sierra checked Ollie's vitals one last time before sitting down to write copious notes into his file. She vaguely mentioned a meeting she had scheduled for the morning, and assured Ollie that the man who had helped me with my wrist would be taking care of Ollie until Sierra returned. Of course, nobody knew that her meeting would keep her away for much longer than just the morning.

As she wrote, Ollie tried to explain the game to me. Apprhaxis was somewhat simple. Each player took a turn tossing the orange ball, called the Appr, at the wooden board while the other player attempted to catch the ball when it bounced to the other side.

The board was divided in half by a thick green line across the middle. Circles of varying sizes were painted on both sides of the board, with numbers inside. Each player took a turn bouncing the ball off of the wooden board towards their opponent. The ball had to bounce inside one of the circles on the player's side of the line. The players took turns bouncing the ball until one of them - the victor - earned 21 points

If the opponent caught the Appr after the bounce, nobody would earn a point. If the opponent failed to catch the Appr, the player who bounced the ball received the number of points that was painted inside the circle which the ball bounced off of. If the player bounced the ball on an area that didn't have a circle, they lost three points.

I was awful at the game. Ollie invited me to play against Sam for a few rounds while he walked around the room a bit to stretch his muscles, but she beat me quickly every time.

Sam seemed more carefree than I had ever seen her. She genuinely had fun playing and competing against Ollie. I imagined this is how they spent much of their time growing up; getting lost in a game, trying to distract themselves from the dangerous world that lay outside their walls.

Sam spun the Appr as she released it. The Appr bounced off one of the small circles and flew off in the opposite direction, causing me to look up just as Sierra placed the folder gently on the table with a worried look at Ollie. Catching me looking at her, she put on a brave face and turned to face the three of us. She picked up the Appr and tossed it to Sam. Then, claiming to be tired, quickly excused herself from the room.

Sam smiled warmly at Sierra, unaware that this very well might be the last time they saw each other. For a split second, I considered canceling the whole trip. I could pretend we were safe in The Sanctuary. The moment fizzled out. We would never be safe as long as Stratus was out there, especially if he had Jax to experiment on. I couldn't sit here and do nothing.

Sam smiled back and returned to the game with Ollie. Ollie was quick to catch the Appr, faster than I would have thought possible, even with our abilities. He never took his eyes off the board. Neither of them ever beat the other by more than two points.

Ollie had not eaten solid foods for a few days, and was craving a dinner meal that didn't come through a feeding tube. Seeing another opportunity to postpone the conversation that needed to happen, I volunteered to bring him food from the dining hall.

I didn't notice that Sam stood up, and nearly knocked her over in my haste to leave. Then, placing the Appr in my hand, she told Ollie that she would bring him food on her way back to us.

"I'm going to freshen up. I don't know if you heard," she gave a mock glare at Ollie, "but my brother woke up from a coma this morning and the first thing he noticed was how terrible I looked."

I couldn't help but laugh at her comment, though it meant Ollie and I would be alone. I couldn't convince myself to delay any longer. Ollie stood up to walk around the room again. His muscles already seemed more stable than they did earlier, which was a promising sign for his recovery.

He sat on the bed and motioned for me to take Sam's spot as she walked into the hallway. Holding the ball, I sat across from my best friend. When I didn't throw it, he made a joke about me being afraid to lose again.

He had no idea how true that was.

I took his hand and prepared to say goodbye.

"Ollie, I promised that we would get Jax back, right?"

"Yeah," he said cautiously.

"I don't want you to worry about me, ok?"

"Why would I worry about you?" Oh no, I was going to have to spell it out for him.

"I'm leaving in the morning with Flint and Estes and Sierra."

"Well, then…" he thought for a moment before squaring his shoulders. "I'll come too. I just need to say goodbye to Sam first."

I heard a faint shuffle outside the wooden doors and paused to listen. A single racing heartbeat. Well, whoever it was, it wasn't like I told Ollie a secret. Everybody would find out soon enough. There weren't enough people in The Sanctuary for somebody to just disappear without anybody noticing, and obviously Barton would know why we left.

"You just woke up from a coma. Besides, they know what you look like, since you beat one of their guys up. It would be too dangerous for you."

"Well, that's true I guess." Ollie agreed, though I could tell he was miffed.

Wanting to comfort him one last time, I pulled my red ball cap out of my back pocket and plopped it onto his head.

"Look after it, won't you? At least until we get back?" I asked him.

The hat was too big and slid down to cover most of his face, but I could hear his whimpering reply, "Okay."

The heartbeat in the hallway slowed down to a normal pace and moved away from the door, down the hall, and out of range.

Ollie and I tried to play a few rounds of Apprhaxis, but even halfheartedly, he was much better than me. We decided to lay back on the bed and tell stories. I told him about the night I met Flint. He told me about the time he flooded the dining hall. Sam came back inside with wet hair and a plate full of food just as he was explaining how he and his friends had been throwing rocks into one of the smaller underground rivers that ran through The Sanctuary, and had thrown so many that the water got backed up and flooded the entire dining hall. Sam smiled and sat next to us.

"All of his friends ran away, but Ollie stayed behind trying to scoop the water back into the river with a cup." She laughed at the ridiculous memory. "Eventually some of the adults realized what had happened, removed the rocks, and the water went away on its own. It took a month for the floors to dry!"

Our laughter died down and we fell into an uncomfortable silence. It was late. I wanted to spend every last second with my friend, but I also knew I needed to rest before I left in the morning. There was no telling where I would sleep next, or when.

Sam reached across the bed to tilt my hat back so she could see Ollie's face. She took his hand and turned to me.

"Good luck. We'll be waiting for you when you get back."

I wanted to be angry that she had been the one eavesdropping on us from the hallway, but I was happy that she knew. It would help her comfort Ollie, and I was grateful that he would have somebody to confide in. No matter what happened in the future, I knew that Sam would do anything to keep him safe.

I gave them both a quick hug and made my way awkwardly to the door. Not sure what else to say, I opened it and heard Sam whisper "Don't get tangled in any ropes."

Smiling to myself, I headed into the hallway and let the door close behind me.

CHAPTER 16
EVOLVE

Sierra came to Estes's room before the sun rose. She tossed each of us a bag containing enough food and water to last a week; two if we rationed everything. Sierra, Flint, and Estes also had small bags of personal belongings. It was a stark reminder that I had come here with only a few pairs of clothes and my favorite book, which was now somewhere in the desert with my backpack.

The four of us made our way down a tunnel that I vaguely recognized. When I felt air coming through a star-shaped crack in the wall, I realized that this was the tunnel Sierra had brought me to when she shared her secret with me. The floor began a slow ascent as the walls went from smooth stone to ivy and then to the rough crumbling texture of the sand we would soon be walking across.

Estes held his hand up, telling us to wait as he disappeared through a small crack. He was gone for nearly ten minutes before he came back, nodded to Flint, and disappeared again.

Flint stepped aside, letting Sierra and I follow Estes. We made our way through the crack and came out into the open air from between two rocks. Turning around, I recognized the opening from the day Flint had brought me to The Sanctuary so long ago. Once we were all safely through, Estes pulled out his key ring and locked the door behind us.

We stood in silence as, I assumed, the three of them listened for anybody or anything that might be part of Stratus's plan.

Flint spoke quietly as we began our journey away from The Sanctuary. We would go straight to Nevada. There was an old government bunker there, which Flint believed was still secretly operational. It was our only lead, so we had no choice but to follow it and hope that it held information about Stratus.

I should have been excited for the fresh air of the up-top, but the worry I felt for Jax, the fear of our dangerous journey, the safety of my friend, and the future of The Sanctuary masked any feeling of pleasure I might have had.

The desert had seemed so desolate when I first arrived, but I found it distinguishable as we traveled across the sand. I recognized landmarks from my first journey, and noticed subtle dips, cracks, and texture in the land that I never would have seen before. Apparently my skills had developed more quickly than I had realized. Even my memory was more efficient, which made me wonder if I would soon remember my life before Hope Street.

We spent most of that first day traveling by foot across the hot sand. The sun was brutal; oppressively hot almost as soon as it rose in the morning. I was sweating and I was sure my face was bright red from the heat, but the other three didn't even seem to notice.

When I heard the sound of a train in the late afternoon, I let myself hope that it was going in our direction and that we would be taking it. I was right.

The train was still nearly a half hour away, which gave us time to run towards the section of track that turned. As the train slowed down for the turn, we hopped on. Estes and Sierra jumped right after one another and landed perfectly in the space between two shipping crates. I jumped next, and felt Flint's hand on my back pushing me as soon as my feet left the ground. With the extra help, I landed easily next to Sierra who steadied me with a hug.

The train was starting to speed up again, and I turned, worried Flint wouldn't make it. The worry was unnecessary; Flint was behind me before I could even fully turn around.

We stood between two large metal shipping containers. Both containers had doors on the ends facing us, but they both also had chains and padlocks keeping them closed. I had felt confident picking the lock to the roof back at Hope Street, but something told me these locks might be a little more difficult. Especially as we balanced on the metal coupling pieces of a moving train.

Estes reached into his personal bag and pulled out a very official looking lock picking kit. Something told me he didn't simply order that one on the internet. It must have been left over from his time before The Sanctuary.

With the lock undone and the chains unwrapped, he pulled the lever to open the door and very slowly cracked it open. Everything inside had been secured with straps holding it in place.

Confident that we had enough room to sit comfortably inside and that we wouldn't be smashed by falling crates, he turned sideways and shimmied through the cracked door. Sierra hugged me again, then picked me up and twisted so that I was on the other side of her; right in front of the door.

I squeezed through, careful not to push the door open so much that it knocked Sierra and Flint off of the train. My eyes immediately adjusted to the darkness, and I moved further into the crate to make room; first for Sierra, then for Flint.

Estes was going to close the door behind us, but Sierra moved forward and placed a small screw in the corner which prevented it from fully closing.

"Haven't even been out for a day and you're already trying to kill us?" Sierra smiled sweetly at Estes. "Let's leave it open a crack for some fresh air."

The next two days went by in a flash. We spent much of our time riding in the back of freight trains. It was fast and kept us out of sight except for the times that we had to jump off a train, walk a few hours and relieve ourselves, before hopping on a new train going in a slightly different direction.

Nobody said much. Flint spent nearly every minute poring over the documents and maps from his personal bag; Estes spent most of his time scowling at the wall. Occasionally he would move his mouth or make a hand gesture that made it seem like I had caught him having a conversation with himself for a split second, but then he would go back to scowling. I wondered if he was thinking about this trip, or something else.

The constant hum of the train wheels against the rails was comforting, and I spent my time playing a game that Sierra and I invented to pass the time.

We jumped off for the last time near a small ghost town. A few dozen houses circled the town center. The rundown buildings were the only indication that life had ever existed there; the town had clearly been empty for years.

We picked a random house to sleep in. The previous owners had taken most of their belongings with them; the only items they left behind were broken appliances and trash. We only had a few days worth of supplies left in our bags. One of us would need to go into a real town soon.

The fridge had been left behind, but was missing the door. When Sierra checked the cabinets for food, she only found spider webs and a dead scorpion. While I was sure Flint could find a way to turn those items into a meal, I did not want to be there when it happened.

Everything showed signs of deterioration, except a small tree house in the backyard. The bright red ladder was still as vivid as the day it was painted by the previous tenants. The leaves from the tree had fallen years ago from the lack of water, but the giant branches stood strong and cast a canopy of shade over the dirt and small desert shrubs that lay below.

I climbed up the rickety ladder and found the remnants of a normal childhood. Empty soda cans and playing cards were spread across the floor, like the kids had expected to come right back.

As I looked around the small room, I was reminded of all the things I had wanted when I was younger. Sitting alone on the roof of Hope Street, I had dreamed of having a tree house where my friends and I could play. Looking around this one, I imagined that a young boy who looked like me had used it to trade cards with his friends until all of their parents yelled for them to come inside for dinner.

That was the normalcy I had always hoped for. Finding out that Flint had been secretly watching over me the entire time didn't suddenly erase the years I spent feeling completely alone.

The tree house had a small window facing the town center. I bent down to look out the window and could see each decaying building through gaps in the dead branches. The wooden buildings were the first to rot, some of them even crumbling under their own weight. The house we were staying in had been built out of brick. Time, gravity, and the sun's unrelenting heat had taken a toll on the brick buildings as well, but at least it was still a functional house.

I walked to the other side of the small tree house and gently leaned over the railing. Though the tree had provided some form of protection, the structure was still made of wood and I didn't trust the walls to hold my weight if I were to truly lean on it.

I looked inside our home for the night.

Estes was sitting on the floor with an old couch cushion behind his back and his legs sprawled out in front of him. His eyes were shut and his body was still. He wasn't scowling, but he wasn't sleeping. I wasn't sure if the man ever slept. A few times I thought he had fallen asleep on the train, but he would instantly react to any change of breathing between the rest of us.

Sierra, on the other hand, was never still. She was pacing from room to room and walking laps around the kitchen. She did not have any tasks to complete; she was just anxious and needed the movement to help calm her mind.

Then there was Flint, his face still buried in the files he had been reading over and over since we left, though I was sure he had them memorized by now. He was convinced that the files contained information to help us locate Jax, and he was not going to give up until he deciphered it. We had all offered to help, but he politely declined each time. I think he was worried that we would slow him down.

The desert sky was pink and orange as the sun started to set beyond the horizon. I admired my teammates from the private tree house balcony for just a moment longer before I made my way back down the ladder. I dragged a few pieces of dry branches into the house and laid them on the floor next to the fireplace, which was also made of brick. It was probably the only part of the house that still worked.

Flint looked up from what he was doing when he saw me open the back door. It was the first time he broke concentration during our entire trip. "I need you to see something. I probably should have shown you before we left." he said.

"Is it the photo of my parents?" I told myself that it wouldn't be. He always told me he would introduce me to the person some other time, or that he would show me later. Now, his single-mindedness wouldn't allow him to prioritize anything besides rescuing Jax.

"No, it's the tag you found," Flint said excitedly as he reached down to the floor and plucked one of the folders from his pile. Despite preparing myself, my heart still plummeted.

Flint opened up the folder and flipped to one of the papers inside before laying it down on the table for the three of us to see.

"Wait just a minute!" Sierra's voice came out indignant. She turned to me and held both of my hands in hers.

"Kai, sweetheart, have you *ever* seen a photo of your mom and dad?"

Her fury with Flint made me feel like I needed to defend him. "Oh, um, no, but that's just because-"

She cut me off.

"You!" She was shouting at him now. "You said it wasn't urgent! I could have shown him *weeks* ago, and now he has no idea what Carter looks like! Or Katherine!" She called him a series of names that would have landed me in the headmaster's office if I said them at Hope Street.

My eyes bulged and I unknowingly took a step backwards. If I wasn't watching it happen right in front of me, I would never have believed that Sierra could explode like that.

She threw her hands in the air and stormed into the kitchen, whipping her bag around and dumping the contents on top of Flint's files while she stared him down, daring him to stop her.

She took a deep breath and picked up a small wallet. Turning back to me, she gave me a pitying smile as she pulled something out of it to press into my hands.

"We were quite a bit younger here. Your parents had just met. I think this should belong to you now."

I glanced quickly at the photo, aware that I had an audience watching my reaction as I saw my parents for the first time.

I stood there for what felt like hours as everybody waited for my response.

"Thank you," I said, my voice thick with the emotions I was trying so hard to keep inside. I needed everybody to focus on something besides me, so I cleared my throat and addressed Flint.

"Um, what did you want to show us?"

"Yeah Flint, what *did* you want to show us?" Sierra stood with her arms crossed, glaring at Flint.

He brushed his sister's belongings off of his papers.

"This is from a file I grabbed a few months ago," he said flatly, all excitement gone after being berated.

At the top of the document it read "Project EVOLVE" and just a few spaces down I saw something that made my stomach turn.

"Patient: James R. Stevens," I read out loud.

"What is this?" Estes asked calmly, though I could hear his heart speed up. We all leaned in to read the rest of the page. Even Sierra begrudgingly tore her glare from Flint in order to see what information he had gathered.

"These are the files I found a few months ago when I was doing reconnaissance work in Chicago." Flint laid out a few specific pages from his file. "I believe that one of the men I saw lying unconscious in those beds was James R. Stevens. This is the same man who tried abducting Ollie the other day."

"Does this mean they are further along than we thought?" I asked, hoping I was wrong.

James moved like a Heightened. If they were able to increase his speed, I wondered what other modifications they could have made to him. What about all of the other patients? My head was spinning, and I could see that Estes and Sierra were in the same situation. We were all rendered speechless as Flint debriefed us on the information within those files.

There had been whispers in The Sanctuary about Stratus wanting to create his own army of Heightened some day, but it was treated like a myth. This file meant that the myth was not only real, but was very quickly becoming a reality. If Flint was right, nobody was going to be safe; Heightened or not.

The ink had bled, which left most of the file illegible. On the back of each paper, Flint had scribbled and taken notes in an attempt to decode the blurry text. His handwriting was not much better, which might have been why he was so good at decoding the mess on the front of the pages. He had been deciphering smudge after smudge, trying to recreate each document. It explained why he had been spending so much time with the small file. He was trying to put together a puzzle and he was missing more pieces than he had.

It didn't take long for everyone to spread out and get comfortable for the night - as comfortable as we could be in our dirty clothes in a dirty house.

I went back up to the treehouse and pulled out the photo Sierra had given me. I immediately recognized Sierra and Flint. She had a few less tattoos, and he had a lot less gray hair back then. My eyes slid to the other two people in the photo. They looked happy.

My parents looked happy.

My vision swam and I laid down on my side, staring at the photo until I fell asleep.

CHAPTER 17
A NEW ARRIVAL

My heart was pounding in my chest. Loud. Fast. Almost painful with the force of each heartbeat.

My eyes flew open as I realized the pounding heart was not mine.

A heart was beating so rapidly and so loudly that I could practically feel the pulse pounding through my own body as the noise came closer to the house.

I turned my head towards the window, but otherwise I laid motionless as I braced for a fight.

I was not alone. I heard light rustling inside the house as everyone else joined me in looking towards the open desert.

There was a dark figure less than a hundred yards away from the house, quickly making their way towards us. The hood of their jacket kept their face hidden from the light of the moon. Even with my enhanced night vision, I could not make out their identity. I jumped out of the tree house and ran inside with the others.

This town was vacant when we arrived, and there was not another habitable town for miles. My palms began to sweat more and more with every step the stranger took. I looked up at Flint ready to take orders, but he said nothing.

The person stood outside our front door, heaving breaths. I was pretty sure that the stranger was on our side, since - last I checked - bad guys didn't wait to be invited in.

"Ah, of course," Flint said before turning towards Sierra and waiting for her to come to the same conclusion that he had come to. When she realized who our guest was, she rolled her eyes in exasperation.

"Oh you have got to be kidding me. How on Earth…" she trailed off and threw her hands up in the air, exasperated as she made her way to the door.

"Let him in," Flint sighed, shaking his head and propping his hands on his hips like every disappointed father in every movie I'd ever seen.

Sierra opened the door and the person staggered through the doorway, panting. They lowered their hood to reveal my red ball cap.

"What are you doing, Ollie? You can't be here! You should be at The Sanctuary." I scolded him as he made his way inside.

He was out of breath when he responded.

"I want…"

He took a labored breath.

"…to help too…"

Judging by the strain in his voice, he had been traveling for some time without any food or water.

"How did you even find us?" I was angry that he had snuck out of The Sanctuary, and worried we wouldn't be able to keep him safe when we got to our destination. I was relieved that he had recovered so well that he could track us here by himself, then I immediately felt guilty that he had actually done it. Most of all, I was terrified of what Sam would do to me when I saw her again.

He continued to pant, though it seemed his breathing was becoming less labored.

"It was easy, because…"

Gasp.

"…Flint and Sierra made…"

Gasp.

"…their plans outside the infirmary…"

Gasp.

"...so I heard everything."

He looked around.

"Is that a *real* couch?" He stumbled over to it and plopped down on the dirty cushions, causing dust to fly everywhere.

Estes handed him a water jug, which he gulped down. Water dribbled down his chin, as he poured faster than he could drink. I couldn't believe he made it this far without any supplies, and wondered if that was part of Heightened training that I had missed growing up at Hope Street instead of The Sanctuary.

"I just waited until you were far enough ahead..."

Breath.

"...of me that I could come without you hearing me."

He took another big drink, swishing the water around in his mouth and taking two huge breaths before continuing.

"It was pretty simple once you got out here to the middle of nowhere. I could just listen for four people traveling together."

Flint didn't put up much of a fight. I think part of him knew Ollie was safer with us than he would be if we sent him back across the desert alone. He also seemed slightly impressed with our tiny detective who was already making himself at home. It showed guts and wits to be able to track down four trained Heightened, or at least three trained Heightened and me.

Ollie yawned, stretched his arms, and tipped sideways to make himself comfortable on the couch. He was asleep before we could ask him any more questions.

Soon enough, the sun was peeking through the cracks in the windows and onto our faces. Ollie was still sleeping off his long expedition from the night before. I did not want to disturb his sleep, so I tiptoed past him and made my way through the front door, and onto the cracked pavement before I returned to my normal pace and stride. With Heightened hearing, I knew that the other three had heard me leave, but Ollie seemed exhausted enough to sleep through a fire alarm.

The sun was still low on the horizon. It hit the ground at an angle, so exactly half of the street received direct sunlight. I took my time and enjoyed the warmth of the sun as I walked down the middle of the road and headed towards the town square.

There, in the heart of the town, was a small fountain in the middle of a roundabout. The fountain was dry, leaving the mermaid statues to frolic in a pool of sand instead of water.

The city's four shops surrounded the fountain. The windows had been boarded up, but large rusty signs still stood tall above each of the stores. This street contained all the essentials for a town: gas, food, convenience, and candy.

Harry's Sweet Shop stood proudly; a faded pink cottage. It was a stark contrast with Mally's combination book shop, diner, and gas station which felt like it was made of mirrors as all of the dirty 1950's style metal reflected the early morning sun directly into my eyes.

On the other side of the street, a small clothing shop lay empty; the open front door allowed dirt to accumulate in small mounds inside. Through the open door, I could see small piles of clothes that had been blown into the back corner.

Directly across from me, a grocery store slouched with its doors and windows boarded up haphazardly. Hoping there might be some edible food, I pried off a few of the wooden planks and went inside for a closer look.

I fumbled through the store and discovered three cans of expired beans and one can of vegetables wedged beneath the shelves. They were not my first choice for food, but I stuck them in my pockets anyways. As I finished rummaging through the abandoned shop, I was joined by Sierra. I could hear her sigh as she squeezed her way between the wooden slats that should have been covering the door.

She had been worried about Ollie's arrival last night, but now she seemed anxious about something else.

"Are you okay?" I asked.

"Do you think he is still alive?" Sierra looked like Flint with her eyebrows furrowed in worry.

"I think that Jax is a survivor." I responded, hoping to give her what comfort I could without pretending everything was fine.

"Yes, he is, but I don't, I wasn't…" she trailed off, wringing her hands together. She took a deep breath and spoke on the exhale. "I meant somebody else."

Confused about her sudden shyness, I asked, "Who?"

She didn't respond, and it took me a minute to remember that Sierra's husband had been taken by Stratus.

"I can't stop thinking about those files. What if they have been experimenting on him this entire time? Will he wish he was dead? What if he really is dead after all this time? What if they killed him that night? I always hoped he was still alive somehow, but now the possibilities are so much worse. I just," she searched my eyes for an answer "never had to consider it before."

I didn't know what else to do, so I made my way through the broken shelves to place my hand on her shoulder.

"I don't know if he is still alive, but we will find out. All we can do now is find Stratus and hope that we can retrieve Jax and your husband in the process." I said.

Sierra turned away from me to hide her anguish, though I saw her shoulders drop as she made her way back through the wooden slats and down the cracked pavement towards the house. As much as I wanted to comfort her, I could not give her false hope. I hoped her husband was still alive, but I didn't even know if *we* would come out of this alive, let alone bring anybody out with us.

After one more cursory glance at the empty shelves, I made my way back to the house with my expired cans.

CHAPTER 18
MY PARENTS

The sun was directly overhead, enveloping the entire town in its heat. Ollie was still asleep as I sat in the dirt underneath the front porch, trying to keep cool from the sun's scorching heat.

The front door opened and somebody walked onto the porch, casting a shadow between the wooden slats. They made their way down the stairs, releasing a cloud of dirt with every step they took. I recognized the flapping of their shoes and I knew who was coming before they reached the bottom of the stairs.

Flint sat down beside me with a huff, causing more dust to fly. He was exhausted. His eyes were unfocused and staring at nothing, with dark bags underneath. I think he would have fallen asleep right next to me, if he did not have so much on his mind. I sat quietly and waited for him to speak. He had been running a mental marathon ever since we left the sanctuary, and I wasn't about to interrupt it at the finish line.

He finally spoke, his rough voice sounding as exhausted as he looked.

"We're leaving at sunset. It will be cooler by then, and the darkness will provide us with some cover as we get closer to the base."

"Are you going to tell us what base it is, now?" We had been asking him exactly where we would be breaking into ever since we left The Sanctuary, but he refused to say.

He looked me over before responding. "No." Then he seemed to retreat inward again as he made mental calculations and plans for us.

Well, it was worth asking. Although he wasn't an Elder in The Sanctuary and his communication skills could use some work, he was a natural leader. I had faith that he wouldn't lead us into a trap.

We sat in a comfortable silence for the next hour. I still had trouble controlling my abilities, and was frequently overwhelmed by all of the noise in the world. I found that I could drown out excess noise by concentrating on one specific noise or item, but it was exhausting.

True silence was nearly impossible to find, so I spent my time focusing on the sound made by rubbing the pad of my thumb against the pad of my index finger. The quiet brushing noise was soothing, and I was almost disappointed when he spoke again.

"It was so much easier going on missions when I was younger. Sometimes I would be gone for months at a time, and I always returned with enough energy to go right back out again." He said.

"You're not that old," I told him with a smirk on my face.

He chuckled as he continued on. "I'm older than I used to be, but no, it was because your father carried most of the load."

"My father?" My fingers froze and I felt my jaw drop.

"He was better, stronger than most of us. He could hear and see things that the rest of us couldn't. We were only able to stay under the radar because he sensed something I couldn't. I grew comfortable, always having his stronger abilities to rely on. I think, with practice, you might grow to be just as talented as he was." Flint said thoughtfully.

"What did you two do? I mean, on your missions back then." I wondered if my dad's missions were closer to the tuxedo-wearing spies I saw in movies, or if he ever found himself in desperate need of a shower, sitting in the dirt under a porch like me.

"We were trackers. We located people who were planning large-scale attacks. Sometimes we only had a name and a continent, but that challenge was exciting. As a team, he and I brought down guerilla groups, insurgents, terrorist organizations, assassins..." Flint trailed off, but I understood where that thought was going.

A chill ran down my spine that had nothing to do with the temperature. It reminded me that dusty sweat was dripping down my face and about to go into my eyes. I wiped it away and asked if they met each other at The Sanctuary.

"No, we created The Sanctuary after Stratus tried to wipe us out. Before that, we all just lived in regular houses. Regular neighborhoods. My father raised me by himself, and his work with the government took us all over the world. When I was in middle school, he took a desk job in Oregon to provide a more stable life for me. He never complained, but I knew he hated having a job that didn't allow him to use his abilities."

He smiled sadly at the memory before continuing. "Every night, I snuck out of the house and walked to the pier. I liked the water at night. If I concentrated, I could see everything swimming around in the water. One night there was someone else on the pier with me. It was Carter."

"Why was he out there?" I asked.

"He lived a block away from me. He heard me open my window and walk past his house every night, and he finally got curious enough to follow me. He could tell I was Heightened by the way I watched the ocean, so he introduced himself. After that, we were inseparable."

"So you knew each other since you were Ollie's age?" I prompted.

"We weren't allowed to play team sports, for obvious reasons, so we spent our childhood competing against each other. A walk to the bus stop would end with us collapsing at the bus door after a three-mile sprint. Sometimes we would swim from the pier to a buoy and back on hot summer nights." Flint had a genuine smile on his face as he recalled these memories.

"I followed him everywhere, even when we got older and started working for the government. Carter was the one who wanted to serve our country. I would have been just as happy working at a restaurant, but I stayed with him. We became partners and reported to the head of the CIA. Then we became trackers, which led to us meeting Katherine."

The sun had moved and was piercing through the slats to shine directly on my face, but I didn't go anywhere. I wasn't sure what had prompted Flint to finally talk to me about my parents, but I was terrified that I would ruin the moment by asking questions.

Making the smallest movement possible, I wiped off my brow, took a deep breath, and continued listening.

"We were on a covert assignment." Flint chuckled to himself, no doubt remembering a personal joke, but it felt like a branding iron on my heart to know that he had been so close with them.

"Carter and I were in Ecuador. We purchased an old car when we arrived, then drove to our hotel. We parked the car out front, picked up our bags, and went inside for the night.

"The next morning, we packed our bags and headed downstairs to grab coffee from the vendor outside the hotel before driving to meet up with a local informant. I was fishing the keys out of my pocket as we walked across the street towards the car, but this woman ran up and nearly tackled us as she screamed something about a bomb in the car.

"A bomb." I mouthed. It wasn't a question so much as me trying to process the story.

"We obviously didn't believe her, but we moved away from the car anyway. Standing in the middle of the street with a woman screaming about bombs wasn't a very good way for us to avoid attention. Well, your mom was right. The car was rigged to blow. She saved our lives."

"How did she know?" I asked.

"She was trying to track down our informant. She knew we had a meeting with him that day, so she planned to follow us to our meeting and then apprehend him as soon as we got the information we needed. She was standing in a small café, waiting for us to leave the hotel. While we were paying the vendor for our coffee, she smelled the C4 explosives in our car."

"That's a specific thing to know the smell of." I said, wondering what kind of job she was doing if she knew how to identify the smell of various explosives.

"Oh, she was no ordinary Heightened. After a few hours with her, we knew that she was extremely skilled. She gave your father a run for his money, and he," Flint chuckled to himself again, "he was not a gracious loser."

Still chuckling, he stood, stretched his back, maneuvered his way out from under the porch, and walked up the stairs.

"Do you think they would be proud of me?" Out of habit, I raised my voice in an attempt to get Flint's attention before he went inside, but I forgot that he was Heightened and would have heard my whisper just as clearly.

A few seconds passed without a response and I worried that I really had ruined the moment by asking a question, that he would think it was a mistake to tell me about my parents.

I moved backwards into the quickly shrinking area of shade, wondering if he really hadn't heard me.

"Yes Kai, very."

CHAPTER 19
FUN AND GAMES

We left as soon as Ollie woke up. Hours after leaving the small town, we made our way down the Las Vegas strip. The street was teeming with tourists dreaming of overnight wealth. I had never seen anything like it, and I couldn't stop myself from staring wide-eyed at every person, casino, bar, hotel, and wedding chapel that we passed.

I turned back to check on Ollie. I expected him to have a million comments and questions about everything, but instead I witnessed a miracle. Ollie was silent. I noticed that Sierra held his hand, and I wondered if that was to prevent him from accidentally wandering off.

He must have been so overwhelmed trying to absorb everything in the chaotic city that his brain temporarily shut down. I smiled and shook my head, wondering how many questions he would have for me once he regained the ability to speak.

We left the lights of Las Vegas behind and walked for another hour before we arrived at our hotel. In the thin desert air, our senses could still pick up the heat from the lights.

Our small hotel was bleak when compared to the vibrant ones we had passed in Sin City, but it served its purpose by providing food, shelter, and a distraction. The other guests were only interested in making up for years of bad luck and gambling losses. This played perfectly into Flint's plan for us to travel unnoticed.

Skeptical of every person we passed, Flint told us to keep our heads down as he led us to our rooms through a minefield of blinking slot machines and cigarette smoke.

It was nearly two in the morning when we finally got to our rooms. It had been a few days since we left The Sanctuary, so we were all anxious to take a shower and sleep in fluffy beds with clean sheets.

Estes and I were in a room across the hall from Flint, Sierra, and Ollie. As we separated from them, Flint reminded all of us to stay hidden in our rooms. As soon as Flint closed the door behind them, I could hear Ollie start with the questions. Sierra laughed and answered everything with patience.

No, he could not lay on the carpet because it was dirty.

Yes, he could use the toilet as long as he remembered to flush. I heard the toilet flush a dozen times before Sierra's footsteps marched across the room.

I wondered how long it would take for Ollie to discover the TV. I chuckled to myself and hoped Flint was able to shut out Ollie's excitement, as I was sure he was reviewing his files one last time.

After taking a desperately needed shower, I found myself melting into my bed while Estes sat in the corner, stoically looking out the window through a small gap in the curtains.

Without making a sound or turning his head he motioned for me with a subtle move of the index finger. As I made my way towards him, he mouthed for me to follow him. And I did. First out the door, then down the hall.

"Where are we going?" I asked as we exited the elevator and entered the hotel lobby.

"I think we both need a little time in the outside world." Estes responded with a grin.

"But what about Flint? He said we should stay in the room." I said.

"We will only be down here for an hour. Maybe two. We won't even leave the hotel."

"But I can't gamble, I'm not old enough. I don't even know how!" I said.

"Look around us," Estes chuckled. "Nobody here cares whether you are old enough or not."

I did not believe him until we made our way to the card tables. Apparently, this was not the type of casino that worried about breaking the rules. If you had a pulse and cash, they let you play. I had one of those things, and Estes provided me with the other.

I sat down next to Estes at a craps table and watched as he rolled the dice and made small talk with the dealer. Estes chatted at length about his family and career. Apparently, Estes was a salesman making his way across the country selling computer software with me, his intern, while his spouse was at home watching their two children. He had a typical family, and his story was not interesting enough to draw attention from anybody else. If anything, the dealer probably wished Estes would stop talking about his family.

I didn't know how to play, but I didn't care. It was nice to feel normal for a few minutes. I followed Estes to a different table. I didn't know the rules for that game either, so I just followed his lead. What started with just the two of us soon became quite a crowd at our small table. Estes would say a number and roll the dice, which would land on the number he had said.

The people would cheer and clap him on the back as he turned the dice in his hands, preparing to throw them. He guessed the right number again and again. It was as if the dice were listening to every command he made. The small stack of casino chips in front of us soon doubled, and then tripled in size, along with a crowd of people who wanted a small part of his luck.

When Estes had a large pile of casino chips in front of him, he lost his command of the dice. The chips and the crowd went away just as easily as they had arrived. Judging by Estes's smirk, he did it on purpose. I didn't understand how he could enjoy losing as much as he enjoyed winning, but there were a lot of things I had been learning to accept.

"Well, we should probably call it quits while we still have enough money for dinner," Estes said to the dealer as he picked up the few remaining chips and gave a defeated shrug. The dealer waved us farewell and wished us better luck next time.

We made our way back to the lobby, where Estes paid for two wristbands that would allow us access to the hotel's unlimited buffet. Then Estes placed his hand on my shoulder and led me to the buffet room.

I had never seen so many types of food in one place before, and so much! There was enough food in the room to feed everybody at The Sanctuary for a week, and that's just the food I could see.

I wasn't going to let any of it go to waste. I didn't know if it was the lack of sleep, my body's desire for calories after another day of walking, or the little amount I had eaten during the last couple of days, but I couldn't get enough. I made my way to our table with a plate in each hand, both piled high with food.

Everything tasted amazing. Amazing tacos. Amazing sushi. Amazing pasta. Amazing salad. Amazing soda. Amazing ice cream. Together, they were the perfect combination, and I wondered if my Hope Street chef learned to cook at a place like this.

"Did you have fun out there?" He asked, gesturing towards the casino, as he washed down his pizza with a cup of soda.

"A lot of fun, thank you. I almost forgot how it felt to be normal, even though this is way better than the normal I was used to." I couldn't stop a giant grin from spreading across my face.

"It takes some time to get accustomed to this way of life. You never really enjoy it, but you find little ways to cope."

"Like tossing dice?" I suggested.

Estes let out a barking laugh. "Exactly," he replied, grinning from ear to ear.

"For a moment out there, I thought you were going to earn us a fortune." I said.

"We only came down here for a little fun. No harm, no foul, no money, no trail left behind for somebody to follow." Estes responded.

The next morning, everyone woke up looking refreshed and energized. Flint seemed downright chipper, probably because he slept far longer that night than he had in the last week combined. He offered everybody stale donuts as he informed us of the day's agenda.

I passed on the donuts; I had been up for several hours regretting my last three plates of buffet food.

I was assigned to go with Sierra and Flint to check out the building and possibly save Jax, while Estes was assigned to stay at the hotel and keep an eye on Ollie. If we didn't return within 24 hours, he was supposed to take Ollie back to The Sanctuary immediately.

We said our farewells and my team made our way out the door. I could tell that Flint knew about my excursion with Estes the night before, but he didn't seem to care. Maybe he believed that my all-night stomach ache was enough punishment.

CHAPTER 20
DAM

We traveled at least a hundred miles away by bus, then continued by foot. Flint led Sierra and I up a large hill covered in sand and brush. The view from the top of the hill was amazing; there was nothing to see for miles in any direction, except a large dam with what sounded like ten workers inside.

No security guards, no cameras, no motion detectors, no gates, not even a "keep out" sign. Our one-star hotel had more security measures than the dam. I was certain this could not be the highly guarded secret lair we were going to infiltrate.

"Are you sure this is the place?" I asked doubtfully.

"Not here." Flint pointed to the edge of the dam. "There."

We followed Flint down to the dam and looked over the edge where a gushing waterfall ended in a giant lake. Sierra seemed more confident in Flint's abilities than I was. She acted like she had been through this before, and as his sister; there was a good chance that she actually *had*.

"More specifically, there." Flint continued looking down at the giant pool of water below us. There was no obvious way to get down to the water, unless we jumped from several stories above where we were standing.

"We're going down there?" I asked as I frantically searched for a set of stairs, or maybe an elevator that I had missed before.

Flint looked nervously at Sierra and then shook his head no.

I let out a breath of relief.

"Not us," he said as he flicked a glance at me.

The moment of relief quickly vanished.

"Wait, what?" My voice cracked in terror.

"You can *not* be serious." Sierra was still upset with him for the photo incident, and it seemed that this was just adding to her ire. I saw why Flint had been nervous to tell his sister the plan.

Flint put his hands in front of him, like he could protect himself from her wrath.

"The only way we can get in is through a small grate at the bottom of the lake." He let me recover my breath before he continued speaking, though my hands were still shaking in fear and Sierra's were balled angrily at her waist. "The facility is undetectable because it is hidden behind yards of concrete."

"Then how are you so sure about their compound being under the lake, and about the entrance at the bottom?" I asked with an obvious sense of concern for my life.

"You have to trust me." Flint said sternly. He was looking directly at me, as if eye contact was enough to relieve me of my worry. It wasn't that I didn't trust Flint, but he wasn't exactly risking his own life with this mission.

"And what, exactly, do you expect him to do? Open the grate, infiltrate the base, and open the front door for you? Let me remind you that he is a *child*." She spoke through a clenched jaw before running her hands down her face in an effort to contain her fury. "We should go back to Estes and find another plan." She said slowly, like each word was its own sentence.

I knew it hurt Sierra to give up the opportunity to find information about her missing husband, and I was honestly a little worried about what she would do to Flint if we left without taking any action.

"Flint, do you need me to open the grate for you?" I asked, hoping to ease the tension between them and assure myself that he did not, in fact, expect me to infiltrate the base by myself. I risked a glance at Sierra, but she had her jaw clenched tightly and was shaking her head at the sky.

"It's a little more complicated than that," he said hesitantly.

Of course, I thought, why would his plan be easy?

"Once you open the grate, you have to swim through the pipeline and out the other end. I am going off of old blueprints, but by my calculations it should only take you about thirty minutes to get there."

"What? I can't do that!" I responded automatically as Sierra let out a huff and threw her hands in the air. Aside from the blueprints being old and possibly inaccurate, I couldn't just hold my breath for half an hour, on demand, in an old pipeline owned by somebody who definitely wanted to experiment on me.

"You can. You are the only one who can. The pipeline is too small to fit a person wearing scuba gear, and neither Sierra nor I can hold our breaths for that long."

"I can't either. I did it one time, but I don't know how I did it, and if I don't know how it happened the first time, then I don't know how to make it happen again." I knew I was whining, but I didn't care how I sounded. I just couldn't do it. It wasn't possible.

"I know you can do it." He placed a hand on my shoulder, meant to comfort me, but all it did was add to the weight pulling me down.

"We need to talk." Sierra demanded an audience with Flint, then turned and walked away from me as Flint followed. They had a completely silent argument, with a lot of angry hand gestures, that ended when Flint mouthed something that made her flinch.

Sierra left Flint standing alone as she walked back to me and took both of my hands in hers.

"Honey, I don't think you've had the proper training, and I think we should find another way, but it isn't up to me. Or Flint, much as he wants it to be. It's up to you. I won't stand in your way if you think you can do this, but we would all understand if you want to back out." She smiled at me and tilted her head towards Flint "Don't you worry about him. He'll get over it and we can come up with a new plan to find Jax and my husband."

At the mention of Jax and her husband, I knew that my mind was already made up. Just because I was terrified didn't mean I would back out. There was too much at stake. Not only for the two who had been taken, but for everybody back at The Sanctuary who was counting on us, whether they knew it or not.

I took a deep breath to ground myself and gave her hands a soft squeeze. Then I pulled away and nodded to Flint.

He came walking back with an unsure smile on his face.

Flint ran through the steps with me a few more times while assuring me that I would be able to complete the mission without dying or being captured. All I had to do was jump a hundred feet into a lake, swim to the bottom, open a locked grate, hold my breath for half an hour through a series of pipes that may or may not actually take me where I need to go, break into a secret lair without being caught, shut down the security systems, gather information about Stratus's evil empire, and escape. Shouldn't be a problem, right?

Flint was guiding me through the process, again, when I interrupted him by blurting out, "let's go!"

I don't know what came over me, but I just wanted to stop thinking about it. The more I thought about the tasks ahead of me, the more aware I became of every possible thing that could go wrong.

Before I knew it, I was dangling over the edge of the dam wearing only my shorts. I took one last breath, gave Flint and Sierra my bravest smile, and let go.

I fell forever.

The water felt like concrete on my feet and legs when I landed. My body screamed in pain and I was disoriented from all of the bubbles around me. I was not sure which way was up until I saw a fish swim past me. The fish's top fin was facing down, which meant that I was upside down in the water. Once I knew this, I swam straight to the bottom with nothing but a wire cutter and knife strapped to my ankle, and a light strapped to my head.

As I approached the bottom, I saw the opening to the tunnel. The metal grate had a large padlock keeping it sealed, but the lock was brittle after years of being underwater and I was able to cut through it easily

My headlamp was dim, but there was nothing to see anyways. I just needed to continue going straight. As I swam through the pipeline, each passage became smaller and smaller until I could no longer use my arms to swim and had to rely entirely on my legs to propel me forward.

My headlamp was knocked off. I could barely see anything at first, but my eyes slowly adjusted, allowing me to see just enough to avoid running into the walls of the pipeline. I had no means of foreseeing how much further I had to swim, so I planned on swimming until my hands hit something hard.

The water current began to speed up and pull me down the tunnel, relieving me of the need to swim. I knew where I was based on Flint's description. This tunnel would end as it intersected another tunnel. The right side led to the filtering system and back outside the dam; that was where the water was pulling me. Flint made it very clear that I needed to go left.

Not only would the right side eject me without gathering any information, but I would also be diced into thousands of pieces if the filtering system was on.

The current grew stronger and became a very unpleasant waterslide as it dragged me down the narrow corridor, scraping my knees and elbows along the sides. I tried to slow down by pressing against the tunnel, but it didn't seem to work. I was on a direct course to the right side until a loose screw protruding from the pipe caught the knife strap on my ankle and held me in place. It took all the strength I had left, but I was able to unhook my foot and brace myself on the pipeline to prevent the current from dragging me further.

I could feel myself running out of air, but there was a small hatch ahead of me that indicated the end of my journey. The opening to the internal pipeline was within arm's reach. With one last thrust I threw myself at the door, grabbed the handle, twisted, and pulled myself inside.

I jumped up and shut the flap to prevent any more water from spilling into the small room where I had landed. The water retreated into a drain on the floor, but the ground and my shorts were still drenched.

I considered taking my shorts off to wring them out, but at the moment I was more afraid of being found naked than being captured and experimented on. Once I had squeezed out as much water as possible with my shorts still on my body, my next step was to sneak out of the maintenance closet, down the hall, and into the security room. I needed to turn off their cameras, which would allow Flint and Sierra to make their way inside. I took a moment to gather myself before proceeding down the hall.

I peeked into the hallway. There were small rooms on both sides of the hall, each with a folder next to the door. People in white lab coats, doctors, I assumed, were reviewing the folders. They picked up the folders, walked into the rooms for a few minutes, then walked out of the rooms and placed the folders back on the wall. If I didn't know any better, I would have believed this was a normal doctor's office.

As the doctors walked from room to room, two men in all black followed each one. The men didn't say anything as they followed closely behind. I recognized one of the men in black as one of the men who captured Jax. If his face wasn't distinguishable enough, I remembered that the pinky finger on his left hand was cut off at the first knuckle.

Something drew their attention away, and suddenly all the men and women in white lab coats rushed down the hall followed by their dark shadows. The man with the stub finger followed his assigned doctor into the other corridor. As the last person made their way around the corner, I decided it was time for me to make my way to the security room.

As I walked down the hallway leaving small puddles in my wake, I glanced inside the rooms I was passing. Each room held one man laying on a hospital gurney, wearing a patient gown. It was all too similar to what Flint had described seeing in the apartment complex basement. The men lay motionless, their gaunt faces turned towards the ceiling. Their pale skin and brittle limbs made me wonder how long they had been down there. I wanted to go into the rooms but, like Flint, I knew I wouldn't be able to save them by myself. I kept moving forward to complete my mission.

I was cautious with every step I took, and I avoided any noise that would bring unwanted attention. I reached the security room, but as I placed my hand on the knob I had a strange feeling that I had missed something. I took my hand off the knob and took a second look inside the room I had just passed. It was the same as all the other rooms, but this man lay in bed on his side facing away from the doorway.

I knew I was running out of time to turn off the security cameras, but there was something different about this man. He was frail from lack of food, but his shoulders were still broad.

"Jax," I whispered. There was no movement. I paused and listened as hard as I could for any movement coming back down the hallway. When I didn't hear anything, I went inside the room. I rushed to the man's side and gently rolled him over. It was him. It was Jax! I tried to wake him up as I frantically removed tubes and wires sticking out of him.

"Jax, can you hear me?" I whispered.

"Kai?" He responded.

"We have to get you out of here! Hurry!" I whispered while pulling him to a seated position.

He was weak, but he was able to move slowly on his own. I started to take him towards the security room, but realized we didn't have enough time. Flint might be disappointed that we hadn't gathered any new information, but how upset could he be if I came out with Jax?

I could hear the men walking back towards us. We were out of options. We could go towards the security room and be caught, or we would take our chances in the water line. I was not sure Jax would be able to make it through the pipes with his full strength, let alone in his current condition, but the other option was to be captured, experimented on, and killed.

I briefly told Jax my plan as I opened the hatch. We both took a deep breath and then hopped into the tunnels. I went first, and let him hold onto my feet. From the hatch, it was a straight shot to the right side of the tunnel, where the current pulled us quickly through.

We hit two more tunnel intersections before the current slowed down. Jax was able to swim on his own, but he was slow and running out of breath.

As we approached the final intersection, our options were to take the shortcut through the filtering system and hope the propellers were off, or to take the long route which would continue gently pushing us out into the lake.

With the way Jax seemed to be losing consciousness, the long way would surely kill him. We had to cut through the filtering system. I knew what Flint said about being cut into a thousand pieces, but we really didn't have an option.

The current grew stronger and stronger as we made our way down the pipeline. Jax didn't have to use any strength since the current pulled us along, but that same current meant the filtering system was on.

The tunnel made a slight curve and I could see the giant blades spinning a hundred times a minute.

I tried grasping onto the sleek tunnel walls, but I couldn't prevent us from sliding down the pipeline. My already wounded knees and elbows continued to be torn up as they banged against the sides. The current was pulling so hard that it was ramming Jax's shoulders up towards my legs, but the tunnel was too small to fit us side by side

The combination of his shoulders and my legs had been wide enough for us to momentarily clog the pipe and stop ourselves from being shredded. We were only inches away from the blades, but were jammed next to each other like a couple of sardines.

I needed to find a way to stop the blades. Jax was running out of air and I didn't want to be diced into hundreds of pieces.

I took the knife from my ankle and shoved it into the blades. The blades started to slow as the knife made its way around in circles. But it was no use. The knife eventually dislodged and shot out the other side.

Jax's lips were turning blue and I was starting to lose hope when I remembered the wire cutters. It was our last opportunity. If this didn't work, I had nothing else to stop the blades of death. I watched the blades spin round and focused until I could slow it down in my mind. I had to time it perfectly.

Moving faster than I had ever moved before, I shoved the tool in between the blades.

The blades stopped.

The current stopped.

Jax pushed himself backwards in the tunnel, dislodging himself from my legs, and I quickly squeezed between the blades before reaching back to pull him through.

Once we were through the blades, the gentle current pulled us along the tunnel until we popped out at the bottom of the dam and landed back in the lake I had jumped into.

I grabbed Jax by the arm and swam towards the surface.

We popped up, both gasping for air. I looked around and saw Sierra and Flint on the shoreline motioning for us to come quickly. Before I could consider the fact that they had taken a way down that didn't involve jumping to their death like I had, I rolled onto my back and pulled Jax along with me as we made our way towards the water's edge.

Flint and Sierra had entered the water up to their chests.

As soon as we reached them, Flint grabbed Jax and carried him to the dry land while Sierra pulled me into the biggest hug I had ever received. She didn't let go as we trudged through the water to meet up with Flint and Jax on the shore.

Jax and I both had bloody knees, elbows, and shoulders, but I didn't care as I laid on the bank and gasped for air.

We were going to be okay.

All of us.

CHAPTER 21
WHAT DOES JAX KNOW?

Although exhausted, I couldn't help but smile at Ollie's brightly tie-dyed "My uncle went to Las Vegas and all I got was this lousy t-shirt" shirt, with matching pants. I was glad that Ollie had fun with Estes while we were out.

Our rendezvous at the hotel was brief; the excitement and questions would have to come after we moved further away from the dam. After all, you don't orchestrate a prison break and then hang out in the nearest town.

We gave Jax as much space as possible in the small hotel room, giving him the time he needed to get ready. Although he respected Estes's decision not to talk to Jax, Ollie's curiosity had him constantly underfoot. Sierra took it upon herself to give Jax a break by distracting Ollie with other crucial matters, such as buying snacks and clothes for Jax.

By the time we left the hotel, Ollie had popsicle-stained lips and Jax had a different haircut. Jax's tie-dyed clothes that Ollie had selected to match his own hid the various injuries on his body.

"Well, that's one way to blend in," Estes muttered good naturedly.

Jax struggled to keep up with the rest of us, even being propped up between me and Estes. Though I was injured and exhausted, I knew Jax was in much worse condition. Doubting our ability to evade Stratus's team, Flint broke off from the rest of us in hopes of creating a diversion.

I was worried that Flint wouldn't be able to create a diversion big enough to cover for their test subject stumbling down the main road, but I quickly realized how lucky we were to have Sin City as our cover. Dragging a mostly-conscious man through any other city would have been conspicuous, but we blended right in as we made our way down the boisterous Las Vegas Strip.

It took us almost twice the amount of time to get from Las Vegas to the small ghost town as it did when we initially headed towards Las Vegas, but Jax's dwindling energy made him difficult to carry. We were still about a mile from the town when Flint caught up to us. He was drenched in sweat from running with four bags full of supplies and a massive canister of gasoline.

"I blew the dam." Flint huffed as he handed the bags to Sierra and shifted the weight of the gasoline.

There was a moment of silence while we all processed his words.

"You blew up the whole dam?" Estes almost dropped Jax.

"No, Estes, I did not drown hundreds of thousands of people and destroy an ecosystem. I had the blueprints memorized, so I blew up just enough to cause chaos without destroying any structural security. The dam survived."

Jax's groan snapped all of us out of the staring contest we had fallen into, and we walked the last few minutes without speaking.

We slept in the same house as before. It was bizarre to think about how much had changed in less than two days: Ollie tracked us down, I saw Las Vegas and ate at a buffet, I went on my first mission, and we successfully retrieved Jax.

The small house was full as the six of us found places to lay down and quickly fell asleep.

For the next three days, Jax recovered in the house while the rest of us explored the town. We were all hypervigilant about listening for incoming people or vehicles, knowing that Stratus would focus his effort on finding us as soon as he emptied his operation at the dam.

Ollie and I explored the shops and houses. Every item was exciting and new to him. When I showed him the treehouse, he exploded with joy.

When we woke up on the fourth day, Jax was sitting with his back to the wall and his knees pulled up to his chest with all of Flint's files spread in front of him.

Flint was able to confirm, based on the little amount of information Jax was able to share, that Stratus was definitely trying to create his own Heightened army.

Jax had still been sedated when they brought him to the dam. He was immediately strapped to the bed where I had found him. Being trapped in a small room with an even smaller window meant he wasn't able to give us many details about the operation. He vaguely remembered the structure of the dam, but we were pretty sure Stratus would have cleared out any trace of his activity by now.

Two men in white lab coats came into Jax's room every hour to take blood samples. Then they went straight into the other rooms, which were full of non-Heightened people.

Jax originally shared a room with one of these people. They died a few hours after they were injected with some kind of serum that included his blood. The white coats brought in another person to fill the bed before the sheets were even cold.

"After the fifth person, I turned away so I wouldn't have to see their faces. It was easier that way, not to have to watch them die." His voice cracked and he hung his head between his knees as he struggled for breath.

Sierra moved to sit next to him against the wall, close enough that they shared body heat. After a few moments, his muscles relaxed and his breathing became normal again. I caught a quick grateful nod from Estes to Sierra and I knew that she had used her special ability to help Jax.

"Yes, but what did they want from *you?*" Flint asked, restlessly.

Sierra looked to the ceiling and shook her head as Estes shot Flint a dirty look that was not nearly as subtle as the kind look he had just given to Sierra.

"Jax, did they tell you why they took you?" Estes used a much less abrasive tone than Flint had used. His gentle demeanor, coupled with Sierra's calming presence, allowed Jax to answer.

"No. They only wanted my blood."

Flint cursed under his breath, something I had never heard him do. "His army," he said as he looked meaningfully around the room. He turned his attention back to Jax. He opened his mouth to ask another question, but Estes spoke first and thankfully stopped Flint from hurting Jax further.

"Did they ask you about The Sanctuary?" Estes spoke gently, ensuring that Sierra didn't have to use her gift any more than necessary.

"They didn't really talk to me. They just wanted my blood."

"Okay. They kept you sedated until you were too weak to fight back. Two men took your blood to create a serum, but they didn't want any information from you." Estes basically just repeated what Jax had already told us, but it still got an answer out of Jax.

"The sedative, I felt like I was dreaming. They came in and out of the room, but I didn't feel *anything*. I couldn't feel my body, and it was hard to think straight. It was like I was watching everything happen to somebody else, and I didn't care about anything. I tried asking a doctor why they were doing all of that to me, but it came out all jumbled and then he pushed a button on the machine and I fell asleep. After that, I kept my mouth shut. Then I was so weak, they knew I couldn't escape even if I wanted to. And at that point, I *didn't* want to. I just wanted it all to end." He looked ashamed.

Realizing how desperate he had become in there, I was glad that I had decided to jump. If we had taken an extra day to make new plans that didn't involve me going through underwater tunnels, Jax might not have survived.

I gave him what I hoped was a reassuring smile.

Estes leaned down so he was eye level with Jax. "You're doing great, Jax, and we are so glad you were able to escape. We just-"

"I didn't escape," Jax interrupted.

He turned to look at me.

"You saved me." He held my gaze as he continued. "I was ready to die, and then you showed up. *You* got me off that bed. *You* pulled me through the pipes. You don't even know me, but you came."

"I knew you well enough." I meant it to be soothing, but when I saw his slight wince I realized that it could just as easily have come across as an insult considering the way he had treated me at The Sanctuary.

Seeing Jax's wince, Estes stepped in before I could clarify.

"We just have one more question, and then you should go outside and have Ollie show you around town."

Flint made a noise of protest which earned him a side-eye from Estes. He looked at the floor sheepishly, realizing he had overstepped.

"Do you remember anything that would help us find the lab where they are developing the formula?"

"Stemtronics."

"What?" Flint, Sierra, and Estes asked in unison with shock written across their faces.

"The pharmaceutical company?" Flint asked.

"Some of the people who came into the room had name badges that said Stemtronics."

"Stemtronics might be a shell company for Stratus." Flint jumped up from his spot on the floor. He paused, his eyes lighting up as he considered the possibilities.

"Yes, of course! Funding, equipment, materials, and the resources to keep it all hidden from the public." He grabbed his files and retreated to the corner of the room where he seemed to immediately forget about the rest of us.

"There was a turkey." Jax whispered. I didn't think Flint would hear him, since he never seemed to hear the rest of us when he was in one of these moods, but Jax's words were able to penetrate Flint's invisible shield and catch his attention.

"A turkey?" He said as he whipped around to face us again.

Jax explained that he had seen a turkey tattoo on the forearm of some of the black shirts who followed the two doctors around. Ollie handed Jax a crumpled piece of paper and a pencil, and we all watched as Jax attempted to draw the turkey. A few seconds into Jax's drawing, Flint rifled through his files until he found the exact piece of paper he was looking for. He shoved it in Jax's face, stopping half an inch from Jax's nose.

"Is this it?" Flint asked while pointing to the watermark on one of the papers.

Jax pulled his head back so his eyes could focus on the paper, and then his face paled. "Yeah, that's it."

"I know what that is!" I exclaimed, unable to contain my shock.

I had a book about geoglyphs that was probably still sitting in the rooftop greenhouse at Hope Street. I explained the symbol to the rest of my team.

"It's a hummingbird. The Nazca carved huge animal designs like that into the ground. They're so big, we didn't even know about them until airplanes were invented and flew over top of them. That one," I pointed to the paper Flint was still holding, "is the hummingbird."

"What else?" Flint prompted me to continue, not understanding how much I knew about the subject. What were the odds that the library would give me their old book about geoglyphs, and that I would actually read it, and that the information would help us take down Stratus?

"Well, nobody knows how the Nazca made the designs, or how they got them to be so symmetrical, but they made like 300 of them all over Peru. *I* think they…" I was about to tell them my hypothesis for how the geoglyphs were made, but Flint interrupted me.

"Stemtronics is headquartered in Peru!" He nearly shouted, still standing over Jax and shoving the paper into his face. "We need to investigate the hummingbird."

Jax closed his eyes, probably to protect them from paper cuts while Flint held the papers there. "Does this mean we're going to Peru?" Jax asked wearily.

"No. You and Estes go back to The Sanctuary. Warn them, and help defend them if Stratus decides to attack." Flint looked to Estes, who gave him a curt nod.

"What about me?" Asked Ollie, expectantly. I hoped he was excited at the thought of returning to the Sanctuary with Estes and Jax.

"You," Flint shoved a finger in Ollie's face, "are going with them."

"He'll come with us. The whole way. And he'll stay there this time," Estes responded.

Ollie's excitement turned to fear, but I think he was just worried about what Sam was going to do to him when he got back. To be fair, I wouldn't want to be on Sam's bad side either.

"Am I going with them?" I wasn't sure what answer I was hoping for. I longed for the normalcy of The Sanctuary and thought I could lend a hand in their safety. I also hoped Flint would invite me along with him and Sierra in case they needed another underwater rescue.

He held Sierra's gaze for an uncomfortably long time before responding to me. "You'll come with us to Peru."

"I might need new shoes. It's a long walk to South America." I joked, hoping to ease the sudden tension in the room.

Flint looked confused before pointing at the gasoline he had carried with him and turning to Estes.

"I hoped you'd get one running so we could drive back to The Sanctuary, but now we'll need two. There's oil and a few other things you'll need in one of those bags." He gestured at the pile of plastic bags he had placed next to the gasoline canister.

"I'll see what I can do." Estes was already walking out the door as he responded. The town was a graveyard for old cars that no longer functioned. Estes had a lot of options to choose from, but they were in such poor shape that I doubted he would be able to get one running.

Minutes later, we heard the distinct noise of Estes tinkering with engines.

"We're not driving the entire way to Peru, are we? That will take a year!" I tried to calculate the distance from Las Vegas to Peru in my head. I had no idea how far it was, but I was sure it would take us an eternity. Probably longer in a car that had been sitting abandoned in the desert sun for decades.

"Have you ever heard of the Pan American Highway?" Flint asked.

"No," I replied skeptically. I wondered if it was a real thing I should have learned about in history class, or if it was a thing only Heightened people knew about.

"Well, you'll have plenty of time to get to know it." Flint replied before walking outside to join Estes.

Just like that, I started my second mission.

CHAPTER 22
PAN-AMERICAN HIGHWAY

Waiting to see if Estes would be able to get two cars running was so incredibly boring. The town was small enough that Ollie and I had explored the entire area in our first days there, and had done it again with Jax once he was able to move on his own.

Jax put on a brave face, but he was still recovering. Sometimes he would sway to the side and need to sit down to regain his balance. On one occasion, he sat down next to somebody's front porch and found a game of lawn darts underneath.

I thought they were some kind of archery arrows until Sierra corrected me. The pieces had decayed so much that half of them broke while she was showing us how to play.

With nothing else to do, we made it work by taking turns with the two remaining darts and one small rock.

Jax made it through a dozen games before he went inside to rest. When Ollie realized that Jax intended to sleep, he went looking for Sierra. Even without my Heightened abilities, I would have been able to hear Ollie begging Sierra to read another chapter from the book he found in the convenience store.

I didn't know why Ollie was so fixated on some old book about a seagull, but it kept him happy. And quiet. It seemed like Sierra enjoyed it as well. Even Flint occasionally looked up from his files to give her a smile while she read.

I walked to the barn of a neighboring house, where Estes worked nonstop to fix two cars well enough that we could drive them out of this town.

The barn had more tools and spare parts than we would ever need. None of them were an exact match for the cars he was working on, but he was creative and capable enough to find ways around that. Fortunately, whoever lived in this house was either a hoarder or a collector of unfinished car products.

They left behind piles of scrap parts that covered half of the floor, and even more parts were on prominent display along the walls. There was no organization system that we could see, but we were able to find tools and car parts resembling ours if we looked hard enough.

Estes promoted me to captain of the search and rescue team within the garage while I was there. I would have done it without the fancy title though, just because it gave me something to do.

"So, what parts do you need today?" The dirt blew around the barn when I walked in, and I quickly closed the heavy door behind me.

"Hopefully nothing." Estes responded as he wiggled his eyebrows at me. "I should have enough to get things running." He added.

"That's great!" I replied.

Unfortunately for both of us, I didn't have any experience around cars. I had only been in a handful of cars in my life, and all of them with Flint. Having nothing else to do, I lifted myself onto a work table and got comfortable watching Estes.

Unlike Flint, Estes welcomed the company. Estes even made a point to remind Ollie each morning that he was welcome to join us as soon as his chapter ended. Sometimes Ollie wanted Sierra to read another chapter, but other times Ollie came to the barn. Each time, Estes welcomed him with a big, genuine smile.

When Ollie came, he and I would talk while Estes continued to tinker with the cars. Ollie asked me to tell the story about the dam enough times that I was sure he had it memorized.

If he wasn't asking about the dam, he would hold up something he found and ask me about its function. Sometimes I knew, but most of the time I didn't. Occasionally, I would make up a ridiculous story about the item, just to see if he would believe me.

Estes never tried to get involved in our conversations; he was like a fly on the wall. A content fly that smirked every time I made up a story, which exposed my lies to Ollie. One time, Ollie successfully told me a lie. Still wearing my red hat, he held up an ice cream scooper triumphantly and announced that he knew what it was.

He then proceeded to give Estes and I very detailed directions for using this item when carving your name into ammolite. Within minutes, all three of us were laughing hard enough for tears to roll down our dusty faces.

Our laughter died down, the joy being overshadowed by our current situation. In the silence, I couldn't help but be reminded that these moments with Ollie were coming to an end. Ollie felt the change as well. His shoulders drooped and he began fidgeting with the scooper.

"What do you think we'll find at Stemtronics?" I asked Estes, half hoping he would lie to me and say there was nothing to worry about.

"I don't know, but the possibilities aren't good." My heart sank. I liked that he treated me like an adult by telling the truth, but hearing him say the words out loud made the risk more real.

He didn't say anything else, and I didn't ask. Regardless of the silence, I enjoyed my time in the garage.

Estes had one of the cars running that afternoon. I pumped both fists in the air as the engine sputtered to life, but I was the only person having a victory dance. Estes simply smiled and patted the hood twice before moving along to his next task.

Flint was anxious for us to leave. He spent the rest of the afternoon troubleshooting the second car with Estes. With his help, Estes was able to get this car up and running in much less time than the first.

Satisfied with their work on the car, Flint ordered us to place our belongings on the front porch along with the remaining food and water. Jax didn't have any belongings aside from the tie-dyed clothing they purchased for him back at the hotel, and Sierra didn't take kindly to being ordered around by her brother, but we all complied with his request regardless.

Once our items were piled together, Flint split us into our groups and asked us to put our personal belongings in each car as he divided the remainder of the gasoline between the two tanks.

We would be driving in opposite directions. The closest gas station for our trip would be 30 minutes away by car, but we would both need to go there to fill up the tanks before we split up. As he poured the rest of the gasoline into their car, Flint directed Estes to divide the food and water.

As I watched Estes place his bag in the other car, I was surprised by how comfortable he was with going back to The Sanctuary instead of on a mission to Peru.

"Don't you want to help us find Stratus?"

He reached out and tousled my hair; an affectionate gesture I hadn't experienced before. "I can think of nothing more satisfying than bringing him down, but I'm our best chance at convincing the rest of the Elders to take action. If we send Jax and Ollie by themselves, the Elders might not take the threat seriously. My presence will be our best chance to prepare the Sanctuary for possible attack."

With the cars packed and the gasoline poured, I had just enough time to say goodbye to Ollie again. I could tell he was trying to be strong in front of his hero, Jax, and everyone else who was suddenly avoiding eye contact with us.

I bent down to give him a prolonged hug. I didn't want to let go. When I did, I walked back to my car with the remnants of his tears on my shoulder.

Sierra wanted to take one last look through the houses for supplies before we left. I stood in the street and waved as Estes drove away with Ollie hanging out the back window to wave at me.

Sierra returned with a tin bucket, a box cutter, and the wrench Estes had been using the most for his car repairs.

"You never know," was all she said.

As we pulled away, I turned around to take one last look at our little ghost town through the cracked rear window. I could still see the outline of the number eighteen above the front door. The wooden numbers were no longer there, but the sun had faded the paint around the numbers for so many years that a shadow remained to show where the numbers were.

We had only been in town for a few days, but the ramshackle house was the closest thing I ever had to a childhood home. It hurt to leave. I laid my head on the window and closed my eyes, listening to the wind chimes play their song until we got too far to hear it.

Flint filled the tank while Sierra and I loaded up on snacks. She placed several bags of water, granola bars, and dry fruit in the trunk while I placed my bags in the back seat with me. After filling my stomach with chocolate bars, shelf-stable donuts, and sports drinks, I made myself comfortable for the long drive south. I leaned my head against the window, listening to Flint and Sierra plan the remainder of our trip.

Stratus's formula was the biggest threat to us. If he was able to create a Heightened army of his own, nobody in the world would be strong enough to stop him.

Flint was convinced that Stratus's trials were becoming more successful by the day, if he hadn't already found a successful dosage with James Stevens. I understood his concern and couldn't help but agree with him. After what he put Jax through, Stratus was clearly further along than we had expected.

I watched people in the other vehicles, creating imaginary lives for them; who they were, where they were headed, what their friends were like. It felt like I was back on the rooftop at Hope Street.

Hours felt like days as I laid in the back seat with only desert sand outside my windows. I must have fallen asleep after the sun finished her colorful descent. When I looked up again, we were just a few miles away from the Mexico border. I asked Flint if we could stop to eat at one of the fast food restaurants on every corner.

"Not yet. Once we cross the border, you can pick what we eat. Until then, you'll have to survive on your," He waved his hand in the general direction of my feet, where I still had several bags full of snacks and drinks, "rations."

I didn't want to admit that I made a bad choice by only choosing junk food and that my body was begging for real food, so I just watched morosely as we drove past every single restaurant.

My hunger disappeared when our car jolted violently to the right. Flint yelled at me to put on my seatbelt as he struggled to obtain control of the car. There were no seatbelts in the back seat, so I used my arms to brace myself between the back of his seat and the front of mine.

Flint managed to pull the car to the side of the freeway without causing an accident. As soon as the car stopped moving, all three of us stumbled out to assess the situation.

The back axle had cracked.

The car wouldn't be able to function without an expensive and time consuming trip to the mechanic, and it wasn't like we could just walk into a car dealership to buy a new one. Our only option was to hitchhike whenever it was possible, and walk when it wasn't.

I tried hailing down some cars, but people were in no mood to pick up strangers. Sierra saw me struggling and gave me a comforting smile as she walked closer to the road. She gently pushed me back so I was standing near Flint.

"I can do that, you know," I shouted to her, frustrated that she didn't trust me to do something as simple as get somebody to help us. She just raised her eyebrows at me, then turned back towards the road and raised her arm to signal to the passing drivers.

I had taken two steps towards her when the sound of brakes shook me from my frustration.

A large RV pulled off the highway and parked right in front of our car.

"Y'all need a ride?" A woman with large hair and cherry red lips flung the door open and shouted to us.

I couldn't believe our luck!

"Yes, please!" I shouted back.

The woman smiled and retreated into the RV, leaving the door open for us.

I looked back to Flint for permission before I grabbed my snacks from the back seat. He gave me a resigned smile, which I took as "Yes, of course you should go with these strangers. Look how well it turned out for you last time." I consolidated my junk food into two bags and waited for Flint and Sierra to finish collecting their bags from the trunk.

Sierra looked up and smirked at me. She had never been anything but kind to me, and I didn't understand why she was taunting me about my inability to get help. I was sure the woman would have stopped for me as well.

We made our way into the RV, Sierra closing the door behind us.

Marge was traveling across the country with her husband, Jim, and their teenage twins, Calvin and Davis. I'm sure the RV wasn't spacious before, but three extra bodies surely did not make the drive any more comfortable for them.

After introducing her family to us, Marge began to fret over Sierra.

"You sure you're alright? You shouldn'a been standing that close to the road. You could'a been run over! Why, when we saw you standin' out there in the middle of the night, we knew we just *had* to help before somethin' dangerous happened!"

Her hands flitted over Sierra to check for injuries as I processed what she had said. Marge had barely acknowledged Flint and me, but seemed overly concerned with Sierra's safety.

I thought about everything Sierra had done in the previous five minutes; pushing me back towards the car, raising her eyebrows, and smirking at me. I felt embarrassed for not realizing she had used her extra powers, and even more embarrassed that she had probably sensed my frustration with her and was just waiting for me to figure it out on my own.

I knew I had been forgiven when she shot me a playful smile over Marge's shoulder, but I could still feel redness in my cheeks.

Marge and Jim were kind and hospitable even without Sierra's special encouragement. Their family reminded me of Ollie. They asked a hundred questions and never stopped smiling. It made me wonder if Ollie and Sam's parents had acted this way.

Marge and Jim had founded a non-profit organization to rehabilitate abused animals. They worked tirelessly, but every summer they took four weeks to travel with their children.

Happy to have guests, they left the RV parked on the side of the highway and shared a very detailed itinerary for their trip to the Darien Gap in Panama. Marge squealed when Flint explained that we were also traveling down the Pan-American Highway.

"How about y'all hitch a ride with us?" Jim added from the driver's seat.

"Yeah, come with us!" Calvin added, though I wasn't sure if he really wanted to spend time with us, or just wanted to talk to somebody he wasn't related to for the next three thousand miles.

They all seemed to agree that we should stay with them for the rest of the trip, but we weren't convinced until Davis chimed in. "You really are welcome. I don't mind sleeping on the floor if one of you wants my bed."

Traveling with Marge and her family in an RV would definitely be more inconspicuous than traveling in our run-down car. Nobody would expect us to arrive in a brightly painted RV. As far as transportation went, it didn't exactly scream "tactical team." Besides, there was also no telling how much longer our car would last even if we spent the time and money to have the rear axle fixed.

Flint gave Sierra a look that seemed to ask "What's the worst that could happen?" When Sierra gave him an answering smile, he turned back towards Marge.

"That would be great. We really appreciate it." Flint responded earnestly.

"Oh, yay!" Marge clapped as Jim pulled the RV back onto the highway. "This will be so much more fun than being cramped up in your car." Marge made her way to the small kitchen and offered us cold sodas.

It looked like Flint made the right decision, because the agents barely spared us a glance as we drove through the border. Some combination of Sierra's influence, Marge's hair, and the brightly painted RV caused the border agents to wave us through without even checking our passports. I hoped they wouldn't get in trouble for that later.

Just like that, we were on our way to Panama.

CHAPTER 23
PINKY FINGER

Jim drove through the night. A few hours after sunrise, he pulled into a rest stop, set up a hammock between two trees, and promptly fell asleep. Almost as soon as his eyes closed, the twins tossed their hiking boots on and headed down the trails.

They invited me to join them, but the thought of Marge's large, freshly cooked breakfast was too appetizing to leave. Instead, I watched as she cracked a dozen eggs into a big pan.

"Do you want some help?" I was willing to help Marge with the food, but she insisted that she had it all under control and tilted her head towards the small picnic table.

"If you don't mind, I sure could use some help settin' up the table there."

She pushed a small box across the dirt with her foot, which contained orange utensils and a bright yellow tablecloth covered in cartoon ladybugs. She had somehow infused every aspect of their trip with color.

She gave me a detailed recollection of the day she found out they would be having twins. I found myself laughing with her as she explained that she had tried to surprise Jim with the news, but nearly burned the house down instead.

She finished the eggs and scooped them artfully onto a large platter before bringing it to the table where I sat waiting. The heart-shaped pancakes sat at the top of the platter and our eggs were made into the shape of an owl perched atop a bacon tree. I was almost ashamed to ruin the edible picture, but it smelled too good to resist.

Sierra and Flint came to join me as I was scooping eggs onto my plate. Sierra sat down at the table and poured herself a cup of coffee with several spoonfuls of sugar, but Flint just picked up a mug of black coffee and two pieces of bacon before settling down under the shade of a tree near Jim's hammock.

Once I got a taste, I couldn't eat the food fast enough. It was so much better than the candy bars I had eaten for dinner, and I was hopeful that my stomach would forgive me for what I did to it the night before.

Before I finished my plate, Marge had already refilled the platter with more food from her grill and joined us at the table. I watched as she made small talk with Sierra about the food, then looked across the parking lot to where Jim was sleeping and Flint was thoughtfully chewing his bacon. I smiled to myself.

It was a perfect breakfast, on a perfect morning, with a perfect family.

It was easy to be around them. Especially Marge, since she liked to talk so much. I didn't have to worry about accidentally divulging too much information because her stories were so long-winded that she rarely gave me the opportunity to talk.

By the time the twins returned, my stomach was pleasantly full. They were chatty as usual, and only stopped to grab a handful of food before turning around and leaving again. They had seen some fancy cars on the other side of the rest stop, and they wanted to get a closer look before the cars drove away. Already full and happy, I thanked Marge for the food and cleaned up my area before joining them.

We made our way over a small hill to the other end of the u-shaped rest area. I could see the cars as soon as we reached the top of the hill.

"Whoa," I breathed. I didn't know much about cars, but they looked expensive and incredibly fast.

Davis turned back to me and smiled as we began making our way down the other side of the hill. "Nice, right?"

The owners were standing next to their cars and talking to a few other curious onlookers. As I watched, one of the men reached down to grab his water bottle from the ground.

The man's pinky finger was missing a joint.

I froze in my tracks as I realized who these men were.

Calvin and Davis continued walking. They made it about ten steps before they realized I was no longer with them, and looked back to see what was going on.

"Are you alright?" asked Calvin.

Stunned, I stood silently for a moment before gathering my wits and giving what I hoped was a reassuring smile.

"I'm fine." I replied. "I just, I forgot something back at the RV. I'll catch up with you both later." I said as I turned back the other way swiftly but hopefully not quickly enough to draw attention.

Davis and Calvin seemed a bit confused at my reaction, but shrugged it off and continued making their way to the cars. I walked at a normal pace until I knew the hill shielded me from them, then I ran faster than I had ever run before.

Jim was awake and helping Marge clean up outside. I gave a quick hello as I ran past them both and into the RV where Flint and Sierra were sitting on the couch. With no time for details, I got straight to the point.

"Stratus's men are in the parking lot. The one who took Jax is *here*."

Flint was wary until he looked behind me and saw that two of the men were already making their way over the hill with Calvin and Davis.

Sierra jumped behind the wheel and started to drive away. Marge and Jim yelled as we stole their RV and left them behind, but there was no time to explain. They wouldn't believe us anyway. Terrified for their safety, I turned to Sierra.

"They'll be fine!" Sierra shouted back to me. She must have sensed my guilt. "Stratus likes civilians. He can manipulate them into believing we are the enemy. Trust me, they're safe back there."

I looked back as we sped towards the highway. One of the men reached for their gun as the other pulled out their phone. All three of us ducked as bullets hit the back of the RV.

The bullets stopped hitting the back and immediately began to hit the engine and windshield.

Hunched on the ground, Sierra kept one hand on the gas to maintain our speed and the other on the bottom of the steering wheel as we hurtled in the direction of the highway.

Although the windshield was covered in smoke from the engine, she risked popping her head up to make sure we were headed in the right direction. The man with the stub finger stood directly in front of us with a gun in each hand. Flint reached up and yanked her back down as a bullet flew past her head.

Sierra tried to swerve back and forth, but the RV wasn't very maneuverable to begin with. It was even less maneuverable when the driver couldn't look out the windshield, and the engine was riddled with bullets. The sound of gunshots stopped abruptly as the man jumped to the side before he was crushed by our newly commandeered RV.

Sierra continued driving as I ran to the rear window and watched the man dust himself off. The other men ran to join him in watching us drive away, though none of them made any moves to follow us.

Once I felt confident that we were not being followed, I made my way back to Flint and Sierra. Things were quiet in the front; too quiet. Somehow Sierra and Flint had switched spots while I was in the back.

Flint was rapidly looking back and forth between the empty road in front of us and the empty road behind us. I hoped they both stayed that way.

Sierra looked terrible. She sat quietly in the passenger seat, hugging her knees to her chest and looking out the window with tears spilling down her cheeks.

Her skin was cold and clammy when I put my hand on her shoulder.

"Are you hurt?" The thought of her being injured caused my voice to come out much louder than I meant for it to.

She did not respond, so I started frantically checking her for blood. My hands flew over her arms, torso, legs. When I was satisfied that the bullets had missed her, I turned to Flint for help. He pointedly ignored my attention as he kept his eyes focused on the road ahead.

"Sierra? Are you alright?" I asked again. She turned her head vaguely in my direction, blinked once, and hung her head.

"Ashton." The word came out so softly; even with heightened hearing, I could barely understand.

"Ashton? Who's Ashton?" I whispered, attempting to match her volume.

Flint let out a heavy sigh and finally ended his staring contest with the road. His eyes searched mine, though I didn't know what he was looking for.

"Ashton was," he started to say before correcting himself, "is her husband."

"*Is?* He's alive? Do you think those guys have him?" I directed my questions at Flint, though I still stood next to Sierra.

"He was firing at us." Flint's eyes flicked to Sierra for a moment, then he gave me a meaningful look before he returned his attention to the road. He may have been done answering my questions, but I wasn't done asking them.

"Why was he firing at us? Didn't he see her?" I asked, flinging my hand towards Sierra.

"He looked right into my eyes as he fired those last shots," she said, her head still hanging between her knees.

Flint reached out to gently place his hand on her knee.

"There is only so much torture a person can take before they break, Kai. After two or three years..." Flint trailed off and his eyes widened as he realized what he had said.

Sierra looked up hastily. "What do you mean 'two or three years'? He's been gone for almost a decade!" She said, accusingly.

"I thought I might have seen him a few years back in Albuquerque, just for a moment. I couldn't be certain, and I didn't want to get your hopes up in case it wasn't him, or if he was trying to protect you by staying away." Flint attempted to justify keeping this from her.

Without a word, Sierra uncurled her legs, stood, walked to the bathroom in the back of the RV, and quietly shut the door behind her.

CHAPTER 24
EMOTIONS RUN HIGH

After about an hour, Flint gave me perhaps the shortest driving lesson in the history of the world before handing me control of the RV.

Sierra did not respond to anything he said, so he cracked the door open. I looked into the rear view mirror when I heard the door squeak, and saw Sierra laying on the ground in the fetal position.

I could say I did not listen to their conversation, but I would be lying. My abilities were getting stronger and I was curious. In such a small space, I didn't even need to focus my abilities in order to hear the soap opera unfolding behind me.

I wanted to let them know how great I was doing for someone who had never driven before, but it felt like the wrong time for celebrations.

Gas pedal. Break pedal. Steering wheel.

That was the extent of my driving lesson and would have to suffice until Flint returned to the controls.

Sierra's anger rapidly changed to despair as she imagined the terrible things Stratus had done to Ashton in order to turn him against her. Soon, her depression had overwhelmed both her and Flint. Flint acted strangely out of character; the careful control over his emotions snapped and he began shouting angrily at Sierra.

Trying to distract them both, I called for Flint's help just as he was on the verge of tears. He muttered angrily under his breath as he stomped to the front of the RV, but in that short distance his emotions settled to a point where they were no longer erratic. Flint seemed aware of this as well, and he chose to stay with me until Sierra had time to calm down in the back.

Flint seemed incredibly uncomfortable about his emotional outburst.

He diverted his attention away from what had happened in the back and returned to the driver's seat, nudging me back to the co-pilot chair. I watched as he stared into the dark road ahead and his pupils took over his eyes. His knuckles turned white from his tight grasp on the steering wheel as the number on the speedometer began to increase.

I realized that he might still be in the thralls of Sierra's emotional tornado, but he wasn't listening to me when I called his name.

Our two ton vehicle bounced around as it sped down the foggy road, leaving me no choice but to hold on and buckle up to prevent my head from hitting the window. I looked in the rear view mirror and saw that Sierra had done the same after being tossed from her spot on the bathroom floor. She held on as the cabinet doors above her swung open and the food inside flew out in droves. The needle on the speedometer no longer served a purpose; it seemed to be holding on for dear life like the rest of us.

Trying to see some part of the road, I rolled down my window in an attempt to break through the thick wall of fog that now masked everything in sight. I quickly realized the error in my judgment as the RV filled with smoke. With my eyes and lungs burning, we came to a rough screeching halt.

All three of us stood on uneven pavement watching a cloud of smoke billow from the engine.

"We are not going anywhere until the engine cools down." Flint said as he attempted to see the engine through thick smoke.

Realizing there was nothing he could do for the engine, Flint joined Sierra and I where we were sitting on the ground with our backs against the RV.

"I am sorry." He practically choked on the words. "I realize, now, that I should have told you sooner."

"Yes, you should have," she said indignantly. "I understand that your heart was in the right place, but that information was *mine* to act on. Not yours."

"I know."

"You will *never* keep information from me again, if it means saving Ashton. Do you understand?"

"Yes." He nodded his head almost too enthusiastically.

Although Flint was older than her, Sierra's rage made her seem like a mother scolding her small child.

She sighed, the last bits of tension fading from her shoulders. "Thank you."

There were more pressing matters at hand like the fact that Stratus's men knew where we were, what we looked like, what we were driving, and if they talked to Marge at all, they knew which direction we were headed. Ashton, who might be one of the bad guys now, is the one who kidnapped Jax and then tried to kill us. On top of all of that, we were very far from our destination with no method of transportation.

As the smoke died down, Flint bent over the engine in an attempt to bring life back into the RV. We came up with a new plan as he tinkered with the engine. Sierra handed him the wrench.

"See? They did come in handy."

I smiled. Despite our situation being an absolute disaster, she still found ways to make it more bearable for me.

It would have been hard enough sneaking into a highly sophisticated compound, but now that they knew what we looked like, it was going to be nearly impossible. Flint decided it was best to ditch the brightly colored RV at the nearest big city and find a method of transportation that wouldn't be a beacon to Stratus.

Flint closed the hood and returned to the driver seat with the keys. The engine fluttered for a bit, but after Flint's continued pressure on the ignition switch, it finally caved to his demands and started up again. Flint gently pressed on the gas pedal to make sure the engine was truly working. When the RV started rolling away, Sierra and I jumped back in and returned to our corners.

When we arrived in Culiacán, Flint was able to trade the RV for an old car. It was not much to look at, but the owner assured us that it would take us anywhere we needed to go.

Any indication of the original make or model was long gone. All that was left of the hood ornament was a metal hanger that kept the hood from flying up while we were driving. After peering over Flint's shoulder at the engine, I was convinced that the hanger was the newest part. The exterior showed almost no signs of its former self. The paint was almost fully engulfed in rust except parts of the passenger door, which still showed signs of the original blue color.

We took as much food as we could from the RV, and several pairs of clothing for each of us. Unfortunately for Sierra, Marge's style was very different from what she was used to.

Flint drove to a different part of town and parked in the shade near a casino.

"Stay in the car. I'll be back in an hour." He didn't give us an explanation before getting out and walking into the building. If he was planning to make money, I hoped he was as good at poker as Estes was.

From the back seat, I watched as Sierra pulled another photo from her wallet. It was her wedding photo. I had a hard time connecting the happy, carefree Ashton in the photo with the cold, unforgiving man who had tortured Jax. Not sure whether I should offer her comfort or not, I just watched as she silently held the photo to her chest.

Flint came outside almost exactly an hour later.

"Don't say anything."

That felt ominous, but I obeyed as he drove to another spot in town and handed Sierra a thick envelope while pointing at a used car lot down the street. She nodded and got out, walking up to the salesman with a bright smile on her face.

Minutes later, she was shaking his hand. Her smile had transferred to him as she handed him a stack of money from the envelope, and he handed her the keys to a pick-up truck that was only a few years old.

Flint drove the car, with Sierra following us in the truck, out to a rural area where we transferred all of our belongings into the bed of the truck. Once complete, Flint took control of the truck and used it to nudge the small blue car into a ditch on the side of the road.

"When Stratus finds the RV, that man will tell him that he traded his car for it. Then Stratus will look for that car. Hopefully his search for the car will buy us some time."

Sierra sat in the back seat of the truck for the next few days, allowing me to sit in the front as we drove through several different climates.

When we were just outside Panama City, she switched with me. Sierra was the only one of us who knew fluent Spanish. I knew enough Spanish to find a restroom and a library, but neither of those phrases would have helped us in Panama.

Panama City was not what I had expected. The black and white photographs in my books made the country look as if it was an old television episode. In reality, the country was covered in brightly colored plants. We left the mangrove forest and entered a modern metropolis with large skyscrapers lining the horizon. It was a huge change from the small ghost town that we had occupied a week ago.

We stopped for food, which Sierra insisted we eat picnic-style in the large park. While it was a peaceful moment, it reminded me of the last time I was in a park with Flint, which made me think of Ollie.

If Stratus's men were able to find us in Marge's RV, there was a chance that Stratus's men found my friends also. I wanted so badly to warn Estes, but being tech-free meant I just had to hope they were safe. It is strange how disconnected you felt from the world when you no longer had a form of immediate communication. Until we made it back, our farewells at the ghost town would be the last time I talked to them.

As Flint started the engine and drove away, I fell asleep hoping that my friends were safe.

CHAPTER 25
DEKE

"The Nazca people built their town in the desert. The coast was only a few miles away, but they chose to live away from a water source. Why? Did it rain a lot? Nope! Aqueducts! These scientists found miles of aqueducts underneath the drawings. The aqueducts gave them fresh water. Without their knowledge of water, they never would have been able to survive for as long they did. It was kind of like The Sanctuary," I finished.

Only slightly over one day away, we began to prepare for our inevitable battle with Stratus's men. We stopped at the first convenience store we passed once we crossed the border into Peru. Flint wanted to gather supplies one last time before we started our trek across the desert to find the hummingbird. While Flint loaded up on water and gasoline, I was in charge of snacks.

Learning from my previous mistake, I purchased three bags of relatively healthy food and placed them into the back of the truck next to the gasoline canister, which Flint had refilled. As I jumped down from the truck, my pockets jingled with the remainder of the money Flint had given me. When I was done, I joined Sierra in the front seat where she sat listening to Flint make small talk with one of the local men.

The man, Deke, was a small-time tourism pilot. He gave the occasional visitor an overhead view of the Nazca drawings, as long as it didn't interfere with his multiple siestas or his daytime TV shows. I would not have believed that Deke had ever been in the military if he didn't have an Air Force tattoo on his chest. Apparently his shirt had retired when he did; he had traded in his pressed military uniform for cargo shorts and sandals a long time ago.

Flint made his way back to the car with a pleased grin on his face. Deke had agreed to take us for a tour in his plane, and Flint was quick to take advantage of the opportunity. We were unfamiliar with the terrain and were not too sure about where, exactly, we were going. Flint hoped that a birds' eye view might give us the information we needed.

The sound of our gasoline canisters rattled in the bed of the truck as we followed Deke on his restored 1950 Indian Chief motorcycle. The lack of effort put into his appearance was not wasted; instead he had poured all of his effort into his mint condition sky blue bike. The handlebars reflected the beating sun. Even following from behind, I could see Deke's giant grin as we made our way down the unfinished road. He obviously had a lot of pride in his motorcycle. I couldn't help but be reminded of Ollie's infectious smile as I watched Deke's ear-to-ear grin.

His brake lights flashed on and off as he began to slow down outside a small building. We followed suit and eventually came to a stop outside what I could only assume was Deke's home. When the dust settled, Deke led us inside.

Flint went in first, holding his hand up to indicate that I should stay put with Sierra. After a few seconds, he came back into view with a smile on his face. The structure was old, and I was surprised to find that the inside was more modern than expected. Deke seemed to live quite well, if the giant television and surround sound speakers were any indication.

"Drinks, anyone?" Deke asked as he stopped at his fridge.

"No thanks," I answered as I took a seat at the kitchen island.

Flint and Sierra also kindly shook their heads 'no'.

"Well in that case I'm going to get ready. There are only a few hours of sunlight left so we should get a move on." Deke's sentence seemed to drift off as he left the room.

Deke was not concerned about having three strangers in his house. We all took the opportunity to survey our new area, however; there was not much to see. Like Deke's appearance, this place did not tell us much about him. The only personal effect in the home was a single three by five photo that hung above the mantle of the fireplace.

Deke was just a young man in the photo, full of life and with much more hair. In front of him sat a girl with big brown eyes and thick wavy hair. She was looking back at him as he pushed her on a swing. I could only assume that the girl was his daughter, but from the looks of his dirty house, she was not living there. The carpet had stains from old beer and the kitchen sink was overflowing with a few weeks worth of plates.

Deke re-entered the room in a fresh outfit. He had changed from his light brown cargo shorts to his dark brown cargo shorts, and now sported a short-sleeved Hawaiian print shirt. The shirt may have been wrinkled and untucked, but he looked downright dapper compared to before. He must take his job seriously, since he was willing to get all dressed up for the occasion.

"Well, let's get going." Deke said as he made his way out the back door and left no time for a response.

"I guess it's time," Flint said in turn. Walking behind Deke, he motioned for us to come along.

Sierra and I followed them onto Deke's plane, which was painted in the same sky blue as his motorcycle and sported the same white daisy on the side. Instead of the sweet aroma of a flower, the plane was enveloped with the smell of gasoline and oil, which left the small dirt runway stained a deep brown color. We could not afford to lose any more daylight, so Deke took the controls immediately after yanking the door shut. The plane began to rumble and the propellers began to spin as we started to line up for takeoff. The remoteness of his home gave him a runway in almost every direction.

I felt enormous anxiety as we rose in altitude, but that feeling was overshadowed by the excitement of being in an airplane for the first time. It was loud, so Deke handed us headsets to help muffle the noise. It was clear that we were not Deke's first customers for a tour of the geoglyphs.

He told us about every peak, hill, and crevice below us. Unlike the clear pictures I had seen in my books, the geoglyphs were not easily seen with a naked eye. If it were not for Deke pointing and shouting as we passed from above, many would have gone unnoticed.

"Spiral. Spider. Condor. Dog. Monkey" Deke shouted out as we approached each geoglyph.

He would connect the dots for us as if we were looking up at a constellation. Much like a constellation, the Nazca drawing didn't come into focus until you knew precisely where to look; the lines were blurred from decades of exposure to nature.

"Up next is the Hummingbird. We have enough time to quickly fly over it, then we'll pass the star on the way back to the runway," Deke shouted again.

As much as I was enjoying my chance at tourism, I was pulled back to reality by the Hummingbird. There it was, the same image we had seen in Flint's folder. It truly was beautiful. Much like the other drawings, the land gave no indication of recent human presence.

Knowing that there must be something I was missing, I calmed myself as Flint taught me. I closed my eyes and pushed my focus beyond the rumble of the engine and whirling of the propellers. I went past the scratching of the tumbleweeds and sand across the earth, and went even lower. The earth below was eerily quiet. There were no voices or sound of human presence, however; it was not silent. I could hear electrical currents running along under the desert floor, and I could feel their slight vibration.

"See anything interesting down there?" asked Deke as he began to turn the plane towards his home. "You all seemed pretty entranced with that bird. Personally, I always favored the Star the most." Deke spoke while taking to the controls and directing us back before dark.

"What?" Flint shrugged and chuckled nonchalantly. "No, it was just breathtaking to see with my own eyes." Flint continued to explain. I could tell from Flint's perplexed look that he had heard the electrical currents as well. It certainly confirmed we were on the right course.

Deke flew quickly, trying to land before the sun had completely dipped below the horizon. Before I knew it, we were inside Deke's home watching him awkwardly maneuver around the kitchen. Flint reluctantly agreed to Deke's request for us to stay and eat dinner with him. I tried to help Deke in the kitchen while he hastily and ungracefully prepared a feast. Every so often, he dropped a pan on the hard ceramic floor, which caused my head to ring. It was obvious that he had not cooked for a long time, but he was not a novice by any means. Every part of the meal was made from scratch without having to look up recipes.

Based on Deke's appearance, I had expected four microwave dinners. I was surprised to walk into the dining room and find that he had laid out a series of meals containing rice, corn, potatoes, beans, and steak. The smell of the food left me salivating, and alerted Flint and Sierra that dinner was ready. Deke asked that we seat ourselves as he put the finishing touches on his homemade sweet tea.

"Please help yourselves," he said as he motioned to the food with one hand, and poured the tea with his other hand. I could see the satisfaction in his eyes as he watched us scavenge the buffet.

"You don't have to tell me twice." I grunted as I shoved a piece of meat into my mouth and placed a large scoop of potatoes onto my plate.

Sierra and I had huge smiles as we picked away at our food, but something seemed different about Deke and Flint. Deke was smiling with his mouth, but his eyes said something was bothering him. Flint had been deep in thought ever since we landed, and did not seem to notice that Deke had set out enough food to feed a small village.

"Excuse me for a moment," Flint said as he stood up from his chair. "I'm just going to go for a quick walk."

"Are you sure? You haven't even touched your food yet." Deke blurted as Flint made his way out the door. Deke tried to stop him, but Flint was too fast.

I watched as Flint closed the door behind him, making yet another of his famously quick exits.

"Don't worry about him." I told Deke trying to settle the alarm in his eyes. "He has had a lot on his mind lately. He does this a lot. He'll be back soon."

Deke excused himself while Sierra and I continued shoveling our dinner into our mouths. I looked up at Sierra between huge bites of food, and I could tell something was wrong. Sierra looked exhausted and confused. I asked her if she was alright, but she fell to the floor before she could respond. I stood and managed to stagger to her side to feel for a pulse, but I had trouble focusing. I tried shouting for Deke, but my eyes began to feel heavy before I could get the words out, and then there was nothing.

CHAPTER 26
STEMTRONICS

I woke up in a small, dark room with my arms and legs strapped to a hospital bed. I could not remember how I had gotten there. I tried moving into a sitting position, but quickly realized it was useless. My arms and legs were bound too tightly; no matter how hard or fast I pulled at the bindings, my limbs remained snug against the railing.

I could see light peeking through a small crack under the door. It flashed on and off as people passed by my room. I tried to listen as they went by, but I heard nothing. Just silence. I tried again to no avail. I was incapable of using my abilities. I began to panic as I wondered what they had done to me. I thrashed my arms again in hopes of loosening the straps, but it was no use. I was stuck.

After hours of hearing absolutely nothing, I was startled by the scrape of a doorknob turning. The light from outside lit up my room for just a moment before a short man closed the door behind himself and turned on the fluorescent lights above me, murmuring incoherently as he read the clipboard in his hands. After being in the dark for so long, the light temporarily blinded me. When I regained sight, he had taken off his glasses and was proceeding to clean them with the hem of his shirt before he placed them back on his face. I watched as he continued working his way around the room, still with his face inches from his clipboard. He must have been in this room a thousand times because he made his way around the entire room without looking to see where he was going.

"Have you been enjoying your stay?" the man asked under his breath.

I said nothing.

Again he spoke, never lifting his head up to look my direction. "Hope you're enjoying the peace and quiet."

"What did you do to me?" I wanted to sound menacing, but my tongue felt thick in my mouth.

"So, you've noticed the enhancements? We crafted this facility for people just like you. It took us years to develop, but we created a sound dampening system that will make it impossible for anyone to hear anything from more than eight feet away. It helps us prevent unwanted guests from listening in." The man walked to my bedside table and looked at me accusingly, like I had personally been eavesdropping on him.

Full of fury at this man, I attempted to shout my response but it came out as a grunt. "Who are you?"

"Yes, yes, how rude of me. I'm Doctor Osborne. I'll be treating you during your stay with us."

"Where is Sierra?" I asked, clenching my hands at my sides and trying to regain my composure.

"Oh, your friend? She is perfectly fine. She is being treated right next door," said Doctor Osborne.

"Treated? What do you want with us? Why are we here?" I asked, though it seemed that I continued asking questions and Doctor Osborne only gave me half answers.

"I think you know the answer to that." The doctor was now just inches away from me. "I'm here to equal the playing field."

He tinkered with the IV's connected to my arm as he continued, "I am just going to help you relax a little bit. You sure are a strong boy. I had to use ten times the normal dose I typically use, and it's wearing off too quickly."

I wanted to ask him more questions, but I felt my muscles relaxing, and then everything went dark again.

When I woke up there were some new devices strapped to my chest.

"I am terribly sorry about before, but I thought it would be easier to get you all set up without any distractions." He said it in a sinister tone despite the unnaturally large smile on his face. It was creepy enough to cause my heart to race in true fear.

"What are these for?" I asked, trying not to sound as panicked as I felt.

"This little box is a stress analyzer. It was created to strain specific parts of your abilities. I built it all by myself so I could discover what makes your genes different from ours. You, young man, are *very* different. I can't wait to see what we uncover." Doctor Osborne was giddy with excitement. He pushed a button on the side of my bed. Just a few seconds later, the door opened.

Ashton stopped just inside the doorway and didn't even acknowledge me as he addressed Doctor Osborne. "Yes, doctor?"

"Please come in, Nimic. I want you to handle the controls while I analyze the readings." Doctor Osborne tinkered with some machines that he had rolled out from the corner of the room and placed at the foot of my bed.

"Ashton!" I shouted, hoping he would snap out of it and help me.

There was no response from either of the men. I screamed his name again, but still saw no indication that he understood; he just stared at me with a blank look on his face. He may have responded to Nimic, but it was unquestionably Ashton.

I tried again.

Nothing.

And again.

Nothing.

Whoever Ashton used to be, he was not that person any longer. I wanted to bring him back to reality, but there was nothing I could do except shout from the bed I was strapped to. Maybe if he could see Sierra, or even hear her voice, he would have a better chance at remembering who Ashton was. I was just a stranger yelling a name he didn't recognize.

"Nimic, please take the controls while I prepare the syringe."

Ashton walked robotically to the controls and sat down.

"Now, you might feel a little sting."

He loomed over me as my vision went dark.

CHAPTER 27
AFTERMATH

Following the nonstop shocks and physical prodding, my body no longer observed a normal realm of pain. I had become numb, and I drifted in and out of consciousness as they continued running experiments on me.

I tried to keep my eyes open, but after hours of continuous punishment, they closed on their own. Immobile and powerless, I was left alone in the dark room as soon as my eyes closed, only to repeat this process over and over.

My eyes had trouble focusing due to the sedatives they had given me. I knew people were coming in and out of the room, but they said nothing and I could only see their hazy silhouettes as they walked around my bed. I tried to ask for help one time, but it was futile. I was in Stratus's lair and his people would never help me. Even Sierra's husband had been reduced to a shell of his former self as he followed Doctor Osborne's orders.

In my sedative-induced haze, there were moments that I thought I heard Sierra's voice calling my name. When the drugs wore off, I opened my eyes and could not see or hear anything until Doctor Osborne opened the door to grace me with his presence and the overhead fluorescent lighting.

"Hello again, Kai. I hope you slept well. Your lab results were *very* interesting," he said, clearly proud of himself.

"You may just be the missing piece in our puzzle." He was insufferable.

He chuckled smugly as he sat next to me for several minutes, checking the readings on all of his machines and writing down the results on his clipboard. With the lights on and my sedatives wearing off, I looked around the room to find a way out, but I was distracted by a new discovery. Small brown dots were spattered on the right sleeve of the doctor's otherwise pristine white lab coat. I had lost enough fights at Hope Street to know the sight of dried blood. The doctor looked up at me and followed my eyes to his sleeve.

"I apologize that I was unable to change my clothing before seeing you, but we are in a bit of a hurry. This," he said, holding up his arm, "is nothing you should concern yourself with. You see, I have been having trouble with another one of our patients. She needed some incentivizing," he said conspiratorially.

"What are you doing to her?" I screamed at the doctor as I pulled at all of my restraints. I knew in my heart that Sierra's blood was on his hands both symbolically and literally.

He had the nerve to look hurt by my outburst "Do not worry, nothing else will be done to your companion. It looks like we don't need her after all." He replied. He took a deep breath and then added, "We only need you."

"So you're going to let her go?" I asked apprehensively, even though I knew the answer before he responded.

"No, silly boy." Doctor Osborne replied while writing on his notepad. I was getting very sick of people taking notes about me.

"We will take care of her in the morning. Now, I know what you are thinking right now, and I want you to know that there is no way out. Like I said before, this place was made for people like you. Those restraints on your wrists and ankles are almost indestructible. Even if you found a way out of them, you would need a key to get out of this room. If you found a way out of the room, you are meters beneath thick cement and could never get to the surface. I do not mean to frighten you, I am telling you this because I want you to know that there is no use in fighting.

The days of the Heightened are finished, and I think you will find peace when you accept that." He said as he got up from his stool.

The doctor made his way to the door. "I will see you tomorrow" he promised as he swiped his key card. A small light above the door flashed green for a second to indicate that the door was unlocked, then he was gone and the room was cast into darkness again.

I noticed something else about Doctor Osborne before he exited my room, but this discovery brought hope instead of despair. His key card looked very familiar. I still had the dog tag hidden in the bottom of my boot for safekeeping, but I had no way to get it unless I could break out of my restraints.

His previous warning about being hundreds of meters underground repeated itself in my mind, but I had to take the chance. If I could get the key out of my boot, I would be able to open up the door without setting off any alarms, find Sierra, escape, and find Flint. I knew it was a long shot, but my other option was to be tortured in this room for the rest of my very short life.

I felt so frustrated and overwhelmed that I couldn't maintain a single thought without it colliding with the next thought, and the one after that. I pulled and thrust and schemed and planned, but I found myself no closer to a way out. I could not help but think the sadistic doctor was right; we were finished.

I tried to put myself in Flint's shoes, the man with all the answers. How would he escape? I closed my eyes to clear my mind and focus my energy like he had taught me. I took deep breaths as I thought about every step I would need to take. First, I needed to get out of the restraints. Then I would have access to my second step, the key. Sierra was also tied up, and I didn't know where Flint was. Our escape relied on my ability to get out of this bed.

I had to do it. I knew I could break free if I cleared my head and focused all of my energy. I took a deep breath and thrust my arms up as hard as I could, but the restraints still held. I could not fail. Sierra would be killed in the morning if I did not get to her in time, and I had been in the dark room for long enough that

I had lost track of how much time I had until morning came. Her future, and the future of the rest of the Heightened, relied upon me getting out of these restraints.

Right.

Now.

I closed my eyes and pictured all of the people in The Sanctuary. One by one, their faces went through my mind; people I had never officially met, other students in my classes, the Elders and the children. My mind landed on Ollie with his lopsided grin. I couldn't let him get hurt again. I kept his face in my mind as I tried again. In one sudden burst, I thrust both of my arms up and felt the straps break.

I bent down and removed the straps from my legs, not sure how much time I had before the doctor or Nimic returned. I removed my right boot and shook it until the chain dropped into my hand.

Still feeling a bit hazy from the drugs Doctor Osborne had given me, I swiftly made my way to the door with the tag. I tried to listen so I would know when the hallway was clear, but it was no use. This facility's soundproofing prevented me from hearing anything happening outside my room. I tried smelling through the small crack in the door, hoping to catch a whiff of someone's aftershave or deodorant, but that seemed useless also. The only odor I could pick up was the bleach that had been used to clean the floor of my room. It was so overpowering that I couldn't smell anything else.

The shadow from beneath my door only indicated when somebody was standing directly outside my room, so I had no way to know when the hallway would be empty. I wondered why our missions always relied on me escaping from a room. Maybe we should add this as a training exercise back at The Sanctuary.

I raised the dog tag up to the scanner and swiped. The light remained off for what felt like eternity, causing my stomach to drop to the floor. As I let out a disappointed huff, the light turned green. With one hand on the doorknob, I knew there would be no turning back once I twisted the handle.

I cracked the door open and stuck my head out just enough to see if anyone was in the hallway. It was empty at the moment, but there was no telling how much time I had. I slowly exited my room and let the door close quietly behind me. I had begun walking down the hall when I saw the shadow of two men making their way around the corner. I scanned the tag at the first door on my right. I went inside and quickly shut the door. I crouched behind one of the machines in the corner, in case one of the men came into this room, but it appeared the room was safe when I remained alone after a few moments.

With no time to waste, I went back into the hallway to find Sierra. I hurriedly shuffled from door to door, scanning each clipboard that hung on the wall outside. I quickly read the name of the inhabitant until I found Sierra's room. I slowly opened the door and poked my head in.

She lay in the bed and was staring blankly at the ceiling. I rushed over to her side and put my hand on her shoulder. She screamed and flailed her arms as much as she could in her restraints. I was worried that her screams would draw attention from the guards, but then I remembered that these walls were created to be completely soundproof.

"Please stop," I pleaded with her. "It's Kai. It's Kai." I repeated over and over again.

After a few minutes, she calmed down a bit and looked up at me like she didn't trust her own eyesight.

"Are you really here?" She whispered as if she was afraid of the answer.

"Yes, it's me." I replied, grabbing her hand. Her knuckles were bruised and there was dry blood under her nails, telling me that she had fought back.

"They made me believe you were dead. Everybody. All dead." Sierra replied as she tried to hold back tears.

Sierra's eyes ran over my face to ensure that this was not another trick, and I could see her slowly accepting that I was telling the truth. Worried about wasting time, I quickly explained the situation to her as I unlatched her from the bed. When I loosened the straps from her arms, I could see the marks where they punctured her skin with needles to put her through hours of torture.

When all of the straps had been removed, I helped her stand up and walk over to the door. She was weak, but we had to get going. They would notice my absence soon, and we were sitting ducks in her room. I reached up to swipe the key, but Sierra stopped me just before I did. She shuffled over to the far wall and smashed the mirror above the small sink.

"We may need this." She said as she picked up a piece of broken mirror and put it in her back pocket.

I asked if she was ready as I put my hand back on the doorknob.

"Wait, did you see Ashton?" Sierra asked.

I didn't respond right away; I wasn't sure how to answer. I wasn't even sure if Ashton still existed inside that body, or if he had been permanently changed to Stratus's lackey. If I said yes, I knew she would try to find him. If she ever found Nimic, she might get us both killed trying to save him.

"No," I answered, immediately seeing the disappointment in her eyes.

"Okay," she replied. "Then let's get out of here."

Hoping the hallway was clear again, I swiped the key and opened the door. Directly outside the room, two armed guards were making their rounds. One man reached for his gun and the other reached for the alarm on the wall. Acting fast, we immobilized both men before either had a chance to accomplish their task. We dragged them both back into her room and shut the door behind us.

Sierra crouched over the men and removed their weapons. She emptied their guns and poured the bullets down the drain along with their dog tags, preventing them from leaving the sound-proof room unless somebody opened the door from the outside. When she was finished, she took the knife attached to one man's ankle and proceeded to strap it to her own before pointing to the other man and indicating that I should do the same. As I was removing his ankle knife, I noticed that the men were wearing earpieces.

"This is going to help," I said as I grabbed one of the men's communication devices from his ear and put it on. "One problem solved."

Sierra walked over and took the other man's device. "Two problems solved," she replied, smirking.

We made our way down the west corridor looking for anything that would help us locate an exit. With the soundproof walls, we were not able to listen for the sounds of footsteps in front of or behind us. Because of this, we were ready to fight every time we turned a corner. As we made our way further and further west, I noticed the facility became less developed. The white soundproof walls became barren, and the tile floor became dirt. The underground aqueducts went along for miles, and even Stratus didn't have any need for so much space.

It wasn't much later when I started to hear them talking about us over the radio. They had sounded the alarm and knew we had broken out. The guards were ordered to clear the facility room by room, and had sent retrieval teams in both directions. I knew it would not be much longer until they were right on top of us.

As we continued down the aqueduct, I started to hear heavy boots hitting the dirt behind us as they made their way in our direction. Our only light came from the flashing lights of the alarms along the upper wall. Not knowing where we were headed, we raced blindly down the aqueduct tunnels, occasionally jumping over piles of loosened stone.

Sierra was struggling with each step she took, and I knew we were eventually going to lose this race if we did not come up with another plan. I slowed down to grab her arm and pull her along with me, but she pushed my hand away.

"Go without me! There's no reason we both need to get caught." Sierra huffed, as she slowed her pace.

"No. I am not going to leave you here!" I shouted in an attempt to get her moving again.

"Yes, you are!" She stopped running and turned around to face the compound we had just escaped from.

"I'm not going anywhere without you, so we need to find another way." I could hear many pairs of boots stomping towards us, one pair closer than the rest. I looked around us for a place to hide or escape, but we were out of options. Sierra sat down on the ground with her back against the wall. I knelt down and took her hand in one last attempt to get her moving. She smiled sadly at me and closed her eyes, apparently accepting her fate.

I would not go back to Doctor Osborne. I had to find a way out. I placed my hand on the wall to pull myself back to a standing position, but it gave way and I fell to the ground along with a pile of rocks and dirt. I lay on the floor next to Sierra and looked up at the brittle ceiling as dirt and rocks continued to crumble on top of me from the wall. Smashing one large chunk of dirt between my fingers, I got an idea and sprung up off the floor.

I ran my hand along the wall, taking note of every crack and large rock. The walls were weak after thousands of years in existence. Hoping to collapse the tunnel behind us, I started removing one stone and then another until they started sliding away with the smallest push. After a few pebbles hit Sierra, she realized what I was doing and joined me with renewed energy. We both began pounding on the wall with rocks that had already been unearthed. I hit it harder and faster as I heard the first set of footsteps move closer.

The footsteps stopped and a gun clicked.

"Stop!" A man ordered. I recognized his voice and did not need to turn around to know who was pointing a gun at us.

"Ashton? You're here!" Sierra responded, immediately beaming with joy. She attempted to make her way over the rubble towards him, but was quickly persuaded otherwise as the gun swayed in her direction.

"Ashton, please!" Sierra whimpered with her arms outstretched like she was trying to hug him from where she stood. "What did they do to you?" She asked as new tears rolled down her dirt-covered cheeks.

"Don't move! I will shoot!" Nimic replied in a robotic manner.

Sierra tried pleading with him, but he showed no emotion or reaction. An army of footsteps was now coming towards us, and would join Nimic soon. Once they arrived, we would have no way to escape.

Sierra's sadness became anger. "Ashton, look at me!" Sierra demanded as if she was the person holding a gun.

Nimic focused on Sierra's face and looked her right in the eyes, but still showed no inclination that he knew who she was. He stood with his gun pointed at her chest, looking agitated.

"Stop calling me Ashton," Nimic said sternly, cocking the gun.

"But that's your name!" Sierra shouted back.

He glared at Sierra as if she was trying to play games with his mind.

"It's true, Ashton. You need to listen to me." Sierra went on, ignoring the fact that a crazed man was pointing a gun at her.

"Lies! Come with me now or I will shoot! Final warning!" Nimic ordered.

I stopped pounding on the walls and obeyed the man with the gun. I began moving towards Nimic, but Sierra stood her ground. I grunted at her to comply but she ignored me.

"Your name is Ashton Miller. You love to travel, read, and do crossword puzzles. You have a scar on your left forearm in the shape of a star, and you love me. That's who you are." Sierra finished with a sob.

Switching the gun to his left hand, Nimic used his right hand to roll up the sleeve of his left arm to reveal a small shiny scar.

"How did you know?" Nimic asked, looking puzzled.

"Because I gave it to you. We were on our honeymoon, and we rented a fishing boat for the day, but I didn't know how to fish, and you taught me, but I wasn't very good, and on my first cast out, I caught you in the arm, and you laughed and told me I wasn't allowed to go fishing for the rest of my life." Sierra laughed sadly at the memory.

Nimic didn't respond; he seemed confused as he looked at Sierra with renewed interest. I could hear the rest of the men making their way towards us. They were just moments away.

"We have to go! Please!" I said to Sierra.

The footsteps got louder. Nimic looked in the direction of the men and then back in our direction. Without saying another word he raised his gun in the air and took two shots.

"No!" Sierra screamed as the walls began to shake and the roof collapsed in front of us. There was a wall of rubble between us and Nimic. I could hear voices on the other side of the barricade, muffled by the sound of rocks still falling to the floor. I took a deep breath and focused on the sound of Nimic's voice on the other side.

I wanted to know if he was okay. His voice was barely discernible like he was struggling for air. A sudden panic came over me before I realized that he was not injured; he was whispering.

"Run. Run now."

CHAPTER 28
HOPE

As the dust settled around us, I looked over to see that Sierra had the same blank stare as when I found her strapped to the hospital bed. I told her that we had to go, but she just stood frozen and staring at the fresh pile of rocks and dirt. I had to take her by the hand and drag her down the tunnel behind me like a dog on a leash. Nimic had bought us time, but we weren't safe yet.

We headed in a direction which I hoped was west. My hope grew dimmer with every step we took through cobweb-infested tunnels that didn't lead to an exit. The dirt barricade would not hold them for long. Once they broke through, it was only a matter of time before they caught up to us.

In the underground aqueducts, we had no choice but to develop a plan as we ran. Sierra was moving too slowly, so I picked her up and continued running with her on my back. With no time to console her, I let Sierra weep into my shirt and ignored her as if she was just a very large and heavy backpack. I worried that her emotions would overflow onto me like it had with Flint in the RV, but the adrenaline in my body didn't allow me to feel anything except determination.

I could hear the boulders crackling behind us as Stratus's guards broke through the barrier and made their way over the rubble. As the small army began to pursue us, I imagined myself jumping the hurdles during P.E. class at Hope Street. I increased my intensity with each and every step until I was in full sprint down the passage. We continued on like that for miles until the flashing emergency lights ended and we were traveling in complete darkness.

My eyes automatically dilated, which allowed me to see the tunnel as if it were lit up by moonlight. My body seemed to have flipped a switch causing all of my Heightened abilities to run on autopilot. We were a few miles ahead of the men and I knew they would be unable to catch me.

As my confidence grew, I heard the rumble of engines joining the men. I was confident in my ability to out run the men with Sierra on my back, but I was not naive enough to believe that I could outrun a motorcycle.

As I sprinted even faster, I kept imagining that I could hear Flint talking nearby. He was not speaking to me, but to somebody else. As soon as I recognized the other voice, I realized that I was not imagining it. Judging by the smell of oil and the sound of propellers, I knew he was flying with Deke again. The fact that I could both hear and smell them meant we were close to the surface. With motorcycles behind us, I could not afford to waste any more time looking for an exit. I had to create one.

I laid Sierra down in a safe spot and then climbed up the wall and began pounding on it with all my might. With every hit, stones and dirt crumbled on top of me until I was covered from head to toe in pieces of the aqueduct. I didn't stop until I felt my hand break through to the open air. I carved out a small hole just large enough for Sierra and I to get through and then turned back for her.

"How did you do that?" Sierra asked me as she came out of her comatose state.

"I don't know." I told her honestly. "But we have to go." I said as I leaned down and helped her up.

We both began squeezing through the hole as the men on the motorcycles came to a stop below us. Just as I reached the surface, I heard one of the men pulling his gun out of the holster. Without hesitation, I grabbed Sierra by the shirt and pulled her up through the hole as the bullets flew past us.

"Are you okay," I asked Sierra who was laying face down in the dirt.

"I'm fine, sweetheart" She responded, trying to comfort me when she was the one who was basically comatose a minute ago.

I could see the plane above us, but they were flying in the wrong direction. I flung my arms in the air and screamed at the top of my lungs but it was no use. We were much too far away for them to hear me over the sound of his engine. I looked around for ideas, but as I did, I saw Sierra reaching into her pocket. She pulled out the broken shard of mirror and raised it into the air, reflecting light in the plane's direction.

They must have seen her beacon, because the plane immediately turned in our direction and dropped in altitude. As they got closer, I could hear Flint giving Deke directions to pick us up.

There was a section of land just a few hundred feet from us that was flat enough for their small plane to land. I could see them lining up with the makeshift runway. Sierra and I sprinted towards the plane, but were interrupted as bullets flew past us.

One of Stratus's guards had breached the hole and was firing in our direction. Without many options for cover, we jumped behind a small boulder and listened as the bullets hit the rock in front of us.

"Sierra, get ready." I ordered as I reached down and picked up a handful of small rocks. When I looked back at her, she gave me one small nod. Ready.

I began launching the rocks at the guard as if I was throwing daggers. I knew it would not keep him down for long, but I just needed to stun him long enough for Sierra and I to catch Deke's plane. We ran as if our lives depended on it, because they did.

When we got to the plane, I launched myself into the cabin beside Flint as he reached his arms out to help Sierra up. Just as she reached the plane, Sierra tumbled to the ground in what appeared to be exhaustion. Flint jumped out and picked up his sister.

Cradling her to his chest, Flint hopped back into the plane just as Deke began to take off. We needed to get the plane in the air before we started to take fire. The little tourism plane would not be able to withstand an arsenal of bullets. Deke flew as fast as his small plane would go, which left the rest of us bracing ourselves with whatever was next to us. As we started gaining altitude, I reached for the earpiece so I could hear what Stratus's men were up to. It was then that I saw my right hand.

I looked down at myself to check for wounds, but the blood wasn't mine. There was a small river of blood coming from Sierra who still sat cradled in Flint's lap. Flint was already aware of the situation, as he had one hand supporting her head while the other hand was pressed firmly against the wound to stop the flow of blood.

"Is she going to be okay?" I asked Flint nervously.

Before Flint had time to reply, Deke interrupted, "If we are going to do it, we need to do it now. Hurry."

"Yes, it has to be now." Replied Flint.

"What is going on?" I shouted confused and upset.

The last time I saw Deke, he drugged us and brought us to an evil lair where we were tortured for who knows how long. I did not trust him, but it didn't look like we had many options since he appeared to be our getaway driver. Sierra was drifting in and out of consciousness in Flint's lap, and a handful of Stratus's men were firing at us from below.

"They have my daughter." Deke replied in a somber tone.

"And we are going to get her back!" Flint added. "But first, we have to shut this facility down for good or nobody will be safe"

Flint and Deke had spent the last day and a half placing explosives all around the compound hoping to destroy not just Stratus's lab, but also the formula. They were going to free us later in the night, but their plans changed once Flint spotted us from overhead.

At that point, I had to question Flint's priorities. They planned on exploding the compound that we were in, but were not sure they would be able to break us free. I was left wondering whether he would have blown the compound even if we were still inside. Thoughts like that were going to have to wait for another time. We were not safe yet.

We had reached around twelve thousand feet in altitude and were flying well above the possibility of being shot down, however; we were also out of reach for the remote detonator to work. Flint told Deke to get closer, and we only had a second to prepare for what was about to happen. I clenched the straps on the door and Flint cradled Sierra tightly in his arms while he continued applying pressure to her wound with one hand and held the detonator in his other hand.

We all braced ourselves as Deke took the plane into a nosedive in an attempt to get down fast enough to use the detonator without being shot at too much. Sierra had gone completely limp, causing her limbs to bounce around in the turbulence. I could hear her whimper in pain as we made our descent, but we quickly withdrew as shots began to ring all around us. The plane was taking too much damage; we could not get close enough for the detonator to work. Back above the clouds, Deke did a quick assessment of his equipment. He determined that no major damage was done to the plane, but seemed to doubt whether we would survive another attempt.

"We have to try one more time." Flint said, earning a look of skepticism from Deke.

Flint gently took Sierra by the hand and tried to nudge her awake.

"Please Sierra, just a little longer. I need you." He said, his voice breaking.

"What are you doing?" I asked Flint.

"We can't get close enough without her help." Flint responded as he tenderly propped her up and continued trying to wake her.

Sierra was barely able to keep her eyes open. She was in no condition to do anything, let alone strain herself by controlling an entire compound full of people.

"No! She needs a doctor," I shouted at them both.

"I can do it," Sierra muttered, trying hard to move past her pain.

Deke took the controls once again and began turning the plane around for the second attempt. He was bringing us in from another direction in hopes of taking on less fire, but I could hear the rustling of metal guns being reloaded below us. I suspected that there would be trouble no matter which direction we came from.

We went in for another nosedive and received as many bullets as before. Some of the men dropped their guns, but we were still being hit with more bullets than the plane could handle. There were just too many of them; we were flying into a small army. I could see in Deke's eyes that he was just seconds from lifting up, but then the rest of the men dropped their as well.

I could hear the click of the detonator in Flint's hand as he hastily hit the switch over and over again.

"It should work any second now," he assured us.

The top of the compound was no longer a speck in the distance. The white lines of the hummingbird stood out clearly against the red dirt below. It was strange to see such beauty be corrupted by the vile workings that were happening below. The loud popping in my ears, however, interrupted my admiration for the giant beast. I thought my ears were popping from the drastic change in altitude but soon noticed the smoke drifting up from the west end of the compound and then another and another.

The devices that Flint and Deke had planted were igniting and leaving dark clouds of smoke throughout the compound. The blasts moved down the tunnels like dominoes falling in our direction, which caused the plane to shudder violently and plummet hundreds of feet before Deke could regain control. We held on as the plane slowly regained altitude and began balancing out.

The hummingbird was fully enveloped in smoke. The white lines that outlined the bird had been replaced with hazy black soot. Sierra had done it! The formula and research were destroyed. I looked over at Sierra to thank her, but she was almost unresponsive. As she laid in Flint's arms, she muttered "Ash…Ash saved" before going silent once again.

"She *will* be okay. The bullet didn't hit anything vital, she's just exhausted from whatever they did to her in there." Flint shouted to me, as if he was reading my mind.

With a piece of material he ripped from the bottom of his shirt, he had managed to slow down her bleeding with a makeshift tourniquet.

"We shouldn't have made her do that," I said as he tucked what was left of his shirt underneath Sierra's head and laid her flat on the ground.

"She lost consciousness as soon as we began the second attempt," he said as he returned to the cockpit in preparation for our return flight.

"But, if she didn't do that…" I trailed off as I considered other possibilities.

"You already know the answer to that." Flint turned back and gave me a knowing look.

"Me? How did you know I could? *I* didn't even know." I blustered.

"You are so much like your father," Flint said.

I could see the relief in his eyes as he sat beside Deke. It was something that I had not seen since our first encounter; something that I shared. Hope.

I sat next to Sierra in the back of the plane and looked out through a small window like I did all those months ago on my first trip to The Sanctuary. Only this time, I knew who I was.

My name is Kai Chapman, and I am Heightened.

- THE END -